A
Harlequin
Romance

D1025402

OTHER
Harlequin Romances

by GWEN WESTWOOD

Many of these titles are available at your local bookseller, or through the Harlequin Reader Service.

For a free catalogue listing all available Harlequin Romances, send your name and address to:

HARLEQUIN READER SERVICE,
M.P.O. Box 707, Niagara Falls, N.Y. 14302
Canadian address: Stratford, Ontario, Canada N5A 6W4

or use order coupon at back of books.

BLOSSOMING GOLD

by

GWEN WESTWOOD

Harlequin Books

TORONTO • LONDON • NEW YORK • AMSTERDAM • SYDNEY • WINNIPEG

Original hardcover edition published in 1976
by Mills & Boon Limited

ISBN 0-373-02013-9

Harlequin edition published Ocrober 1976

Printed in U.S.A.

CHAPTER ONE

In the shimmering gold of early evening, the white house with its parallel gables and long verandah looked as charming as Emma had remembered when she had last seen it five years ago. The grapevine, that was almost as old as the house itself, twined its gnarled roots at the base of the stone pillars and flaunted its young green leaves upon the supporting frame above.

'Nice place,' said Mr. Thomas, the driver of the hired car. 'Haven't seen it before. I'm new here. Staying with friends, are you?'

'No, it belonged to a relative. It's been left to me.'

'Is that so? Well, you're the lucky one, aren't you?'

He turned in his seat and regarded Emma with some respect. She was worth looking at, he thought. Lovely figure, slender, yet curved in all the right places, nice skin, delicate and clear, not freckled like the kind you saw on so many redheads. Looked smashing with those dark blue eyes and black lashes. Small straight nose, full smiling mouth, firm chin. Mind of her own, shouldn't wonder. Expects to get her own way and does too. Look at the way she had persuaded him to drive thirty miles after a busy day when all he had wanted to do was to pack it in and go home to have his supper. Charming way she had done it too, but he was always a sucker for an English accent. Came from London, she said, a long way from this little half-forgotten valley in the Eastern Cape.

'Who's living here, then? Is anyone expecting you?'

'I think there is an old African woman keeping it in order,' Emma told him. 'Unfortunately Mr. Johnson, the attorney, doesn't seem to have received my letter saying when to expect me – there's been a postal strike, you know. So when I called at his office, he had gone away and won't be back until tomorrow. His African assistant said I wouldn't need a key, that the house was open.'

'That's all right, then. So long as someone's there. Wouldn't like to leave you alone here. It will be dark soon. I'll just help you with your case. Travel light, don't you?'

'I flew here as soon as I heard about it. I stayed here for six months five years ago and I've longed to come back ever since.'

'But you must have been only a child then.'

'Sixteen. I'll be twenty-one soon.'

Standing on the verandah, waiting impatiently for the driver to be finished with his chatting and be gone, Emma smelled again the heavy almondy fragrance of the huge blossoming pear tree that overshadowed the house. Against the darkening blue of the South African sky, the clusters were dazzling white and a few late bees were still bumbling amongst the flowers, drunk with their richness.

'Have you just come to look over the place? Not thinking of running the farm yourself, are you?'

'Why not?' asked Emma.

Mr. Thomas was taken aback by the clear challenge of the large blue eyes and the firm set of her chin. Spunky, he thought. One of these modern ones.

'An orange farm takes a bit of experience, I believe,' he said. 'You need rain at the right time, and we don't always get it. So you need money for dams and God knows what else. And money doesn't grow on trees, you know.'

'No, but oranges do,' replied Emma. 'I'm hoping they will for me. Thank you very much for bringing me here, Mr. Thomas. I gave you the fare, didn't I? I'll phone you when I need you again.'

'Yes, do that. It'll be a pleasure any time. Well, good luck, lassie, you'll need it.'

He strolled back to the car shaking his head. Comes from England. Spent six months here when she was sixteen. What can she know about oranges? Oh, well, perhaps she's got some capital. And she'll need it to tide her over the bad patches.

Emma crossed the worn grey stones of the verandah and put her hands on the door, smoothing the brown wood as if she were caressing the sunwarmed body of a lover. Oh, she was glad to be alone, to savour the joy of returning to this place she had so loved. And now, on the evening breeze, she could smell the heady scent of orange blossom – or was she so thrilled that she was only imagining it?

Distant blue hills enclosed the sweeping valley that was covered with bush, sun-dried by the winter drought. There was not another house to be seen for miles. Yes, thanks be, during the five years she had been away the trees had grown and even Heron's Creek was invisible. She frowned as she saw a wisp of blue smoke wafting through the dark clump of trees that hid the house of her nearest neighbour. That was where Jared Wells had lived. But maybe no more. Long ago she had heard he had gone to Australia. Certainly, if he had continued in the way he seemed to be going, he might have sold the farm to recoup his losses. Five years was a long time – she hoped long enough to have directed his course elsewhere. For she hoped never to have to meet him again. How foolish you can be when you are a teenager? she thought. But I'm a big girl now, older and wiser.

The shining doorknob gave under her hand and she let herself into the wide hallway. It was all as it had been, the worn Persian rugs that generations of dogs had slept on, the ancient monk's bench of black oak, the huge copper jug with an arrangement of dried proteas and heath, still polished as only Rosie knew how. The high black beams defined the shape of the roof and a curving stairway led upwards to the second storey.

On the left was the door that led into the living-room. Emma went inside and walked over the gleaming yellow-wood floor, across the worn sage green carpet, to stand at the window gazing out at the well-remembered view of sweeping farmlands, rows and rows of dark green orange trees, regular as soldiers, and, in the distance, the blue mountains of Africa, hazy in the swiftly descending darkness. Five years had added to the room's shabbiness, but there was still the homely atmosphere, the wide stone fireplace, the couch covered with a kaross made of springbok pelts, the deep armchairs covered in oatmeal tweed, the floor-length curtains handwoven of natural mohair. There to the side of the fireplace was her uncle's red leather chair with its brass studs, and, how extraordinary and touching, a pipe was still standing against the ashtray.

She wandered across the hall to the dining-room and saw again the long stinkwood table and the chairs with their hide thongs crisscrossed to form the backs and seats. The silver épergne still stood on the vast sideboard together with the cups that cattle, long dead now, had won at shows. And on the walls were the portraits of her ancestors, badly executed in pastels and oils, doubtless created by some travelling artist and miraculously preserved through all the Kaffir wars that had harassed those early settlers.

There was no one in the kitchen. Rosie and her helper, she supposed, had gone to their separate living place some way from the house. They had not known she was coming, of course. The kitchen was as she remembered it, not modernized at all, the floor of stone that struck cold underneath the feet, the stove a wood-burning one, huge and metallic on its raised platform. The open shelves were neatly ranged with old metal pots, the old-fashioned sink scrubbed clean and the wooden table in the centre of the room bleached white and scarred from much use.

She remembered that in spite of the Victorian set-up there was always plenty of hot water, and that at the moment was what she needed most. After the long plane journey it would be heavenly to soak in a bath, and that was what she intended to do first. Supper could wait. Doubtless there would be eggs and coffee in the pantry and she would not disturb the servants tonight. No, for this evening she longed to savour the joy of being back entirely on her own.

Taking her cream suitcase, she slowly climbed the stairs, feeling under her hands the smooth mahogany of the balustrade that some settler carpenter had decorated with stags' heads, a compliment no doubt to the Scottish owner. How pleasant it all was, not a very big place as South African farmhouses go, but giving an impression of spaciousness, each room high and cool and graciously proportioned.

She hesitated at the door of the main bedroom. No, she would not go in. It would bring back too many memories of its previous owner, dear Uncle Mac, with his grizzled hair and startlingly blue eyes that could change in an instant from dour solemnity to an expression of wry twinkling humour. She would face that tomorrow. For tonight she would go back to her old room in the little suite that her uncle had had prepared for their previous visit. Two rooms had interleading doors into a smaller closet, so he had converted this into a bathroom, very convenient for Emma and her mother.

Emma smiled when she went in to the room that had been hers, for she remembered what fun she and her mother had had when Uncle Mac had suggested that they should redecorate it in a more feminine fashion. It was a trifle girlish for her present taste, white furniture and a yellow quilt and a wallpaper of yellow roses festooning the walls, for, as a redhead, she had rebelled at her mother's desire for pink. She sighed now, thinking of

9

her mother's remarriage. They would never again have the fun and companionship they had enjoyed when she was younger, but she could not resent her mother's pre-occupation with her new life.

She did not unpack but took from her case fresh under-wear, a pair of nutmeg brown slacks and a top of cream jersey, and, leaving them on the bed, went in to inves-tigate the bathroom. Everything was in perfect order, the daffodil yellow tiles sparkling. She turned the crystal taps and hot water gushed into the deep bath. In the cupboard she found large fluffy lemon towels and there was a tablet of sandalwood soap on the washbasin together with a razor no doubt left behind by some long-ago guest. She lost no time in undressing and stepped with a sigh of satisfaction into the water. The fragrant soap seemed to wash away the last of the travel weariness and she lay back in a blissful dream, idly splashing the warm water over her slim, curved body.

She felt so happy to be back, although of course she realized she was not a young girl on holiday but a grown woman with the heavy task before her of running the farm. But she would leave thoughts of that until tomorrow when she had interviewed Mr. Johnson, the attorney, and could find out more about it. This evening in her first hours at Sunglow she would recall only the many hours of happiness she had known here five years ago.

But as soon as she had made this firm decision, she started thinking about Jared, and that episode was cer-tainly not a happy memory. She must not think about it. She tried to close her mind to it and remember everything else about her holiday that had been good – and it had been utter bliss until the last weeks. She had been sixteen, and until then had been unsure of her appearance, the bright red hair about which people teased her, the huge eyes that looked too big for her small pale face, and she was very conscious of the new swell of her breasts below the delicate hollows of her throat and the curve of her hips beneath the slender waist.

But here in this sunlit corner of Africa, she had blossomed into beauty, become more confident and found that she had attained a certain delightful power over the boys of her own age. They had vied with each other to escort her to parties, to play tennis and ride with her. She tried to remember who they had been, for some of them must still live here, of course, but she could not recall any of them clearly. In her mind there was a jumble of sun-burned faces, some with dark hair, some sun-streaked blond, all with hefty brown limbs and broad shoulders, but the only face that was clear was that of Jared, the man she had first loved, then hated with all the terrible emotions of a very young girl.

Five years ago Jared Wells must have been over thirty already – and that should have put me off, thought Emma, wiggling her foot to turn the tap and heat up the bath again. Most of the parties at the farms were for all ages and she had noticed him straight away. Who could help it, for he was certainly good-looking in a reckless, sinister way, and or course that's just the sort of type that appeals to adolescents, thought Emma, from the height now of her twenty-one years. Black hair, dark eyes, the wild arrogance of something untamed about him. While she danced the nights away with her succession of sun-tanned young men, he was always there in the back-ground, laughing in a group of older people, the centre of the crowd, a silver tankard in his hand, or else dancing with the more sophisticated women, usually the married ones. But while everyone else was making a fuss of her, spoiling her, flattering her, he did not seem to notice her at all.

This annoyed her. She was at that stage where she was interested in testing this strange new power she seemed to have acquired over men and here was one, a very attractive man, who ignored her completely. Even the older men looked at her these days as if they wished they were a few years younger, but he looked through her as if she did not exist.

The test came when she was invited to a dance at a farm some miles away and asked to bring a partner. She would make him notice her, she decided. Instead of asking one of her group, she would ask Jared. She did not tell her mother or her uncle of her intention. Her uncle, she had realized, had a soft spot for Jared, but she did not know whether it would extend to approving of his escorting his niece to a dance. Her mother, she knew, would be hesitant about entrusting her daughter to a man with Jared's reputation.

Even among the young people of her own crowd Emma had heard talk about him. He was the only son of rich parents; his mother had died when he was very young and he had been brought up by an indulgent father. Now he had inherited Heron's Creek, he seemed determined to run through his wealth as quickly as possible by leading a wild life. He travelled a lot and left the farm in the care of managers who feathered their own nests. He was rumoured to be involved with more than one married woman. But to Emma this all lent glamour to him. She would like to know more about men, especially Jared. Her uncle and mother were both indulgent to her, and if she had already asked him they could hardly forbid her to go.

Her opportunity came one day when she was out riding. Deliberately she had ridden to the edge of the boundaries of Sunglow where it adjoined Heron's Creek. A stream divided the properties and sometimes she had seen him riding too, a distant dark figure on a black horse. She tethered her own mount and sat waiting at the ford, the sun gleaming on her copper-bright hair that was tied back with a black bow. She was wearing faded blue jeans and a clinging shirt that she had left provocatively unbuttoned. She sat on a flat rock and all around her was the warm smell of Africa, the spicy fragrance of wild grasses and herbs bruised by her horse's hoofs. She had been there for half an hour sucking a straw and idly dreaming when she saw the black horse with its white blaze and its rider clad only in tight black jeans as he rode like a matador towards the stream. Something deep inside her quivered like a captive bird, but she felt determined to go through with her plan.

'Hi!' she shouted, standing up and waving.

'Hi to you too, whoever you are,' he shouted, shading his eyes in order to see her better. 'Oh, hello, it's you.'

He brought his horse splashing across the stream and left it drinking while he descended and came towards her. Now that she saw him at close quarters, she felt her nerve failing. But at least she seemed to have his full attention, for he was smiling down at her, his eyes looking her up and down and finally concentrating on her face, until she felt her own blue eyes were drowning in the depths of a warm dark sea. His head was bare, the springing black hair the same colour as the fierce wing-shaped eyebrows and the curling tendrils on his bronze-brown chest. In her sixteen years Emma had never before realized that a woman could be so conscious of a male body and of the sensuous smell of it that was as individual as that of the crushed herbs underfoot.

She gestured to the small haversack she had been carrying. Anything to keep him there.

'I've got some apples and lemonade here. I wondered whether you would like some.'

He looked rather amused, and Emma supposed he thought her childish, but she could not think of any other way of making him stay. She poured out the lemonade, wishing she had thought of bringing beer and offered him an apple.

'Well, Eve, is it safe, do you think, for me to take this?'

She did not know how to meet that quizzical stare.

'Would you like it peeled?' she asked. Oh, why couldn't she think of something exciting to say, something that would attract and hold him?

'No; unlike my women, I prefer my apples dressed.'

He took the apple she handed to him and bit into it. She noticed how white and even his teeth were. Goodness, he even looked attractive crunching an apple!

'Is there room for me on that rock, do you think?'

He sat beside her on the small flat stone and she was very conscious of the warmth of his thigh against the thin fabric of her jeans. But she did not move away. She felt his eyes on her and in a sudden panic about her appearance she fastened another button on the open neck of her shirt.

'Why are you doing that?' he asked. 'You look charming. Surely all young girls with lovely bodies know how alluring they look with tight jeans and their shirts unbuttoned? Sorry, perhaps I shouldn't say things like that. I guess I must guard my tongue with someone as young as you.'

'I'm sixteen,' Emma asserted, unfastening the button. He threw back his head and laughed.

'What a great age! Oh, Emma – that's your name, isn't it? How does it feel to be sixteen with all your life before you?'

'It sometimes feels very uncomfortable,' she confessed. 'Why?'

'Because you don't know enough. You want people to like you and you don't know how to make them.'

'By people I gather you mean boys. Well, Emma, looking at you I shouldn't worry on that score.'

'Truly? Do you think I'm attractive, Jared?'

One of the girls at school had said that if you first lowered your lids and then opened your eyes as wide as possible this was known to have a quite devastating effect on men. Emma tried it now. Jared's dark eyes met hers with a steady regard.

'I think you're a minx, Emma, and I hate to think of the number of hearts you're going to break in a few years' time.'

'Oh, Jared, please don't talk to me as if you were years and years older than I!' she begged.

'But, my dear girl, I am.'

'I hate people to be coy with me about being young.'

'It won't last for ever, Emma, believe me.'

'Jared, would you do something for me?' she asked suddenly.

'That, I can't help thinking, is a loaded question. What do you want me to do?'

She turned the full blaze of her dark blue eyes upon him.

'I need a partner for the dance at Seventeen Oaks Farm. Would you come with me?'

'My dear child . . .'

'I told you I am not a child!' Emma snapped.

'That's perfectly true, Emma. I apologize.'

She could feel his eyes on her, the intent dark gaze that made her quiveringly aware of her own body, an awareness she had never felt before, her glowing hair vibrant in the sunlight, her full soft mouth so near to his, the creamy skin where her shirt half concealed, half revealed the curves of her young breasts. He put out his hand and her heart throbbed with suffocating excitement as he touched her hair.

'Silk and fire,' he murmured. 'You really are a lovely girl, Emma.'

At his touch she felt as if an electric shock had charged through the sensitive tendrils of her copper hair, and perhaps he had felt something too, for he dropped his hand as if it had burned him.

'What about all these boys I've noticed dancing attendance on you, Emma? Aren't they queueing to take you to this party?'

So he had noticed her! She became even more determined he should be the one to accompany her.

'They bore me,' she shrugged. 'They can't talk about anything but rugby and buying cattle.'

'And how do you know I don't? Why me, Emma, for God's sake?'

'You are different, Jared.'

He threw back his head and laughed, and she noticed once more how it made his chest muscles ripple beneath the bronze skin.

'I'll say I am! In the first place I'm almost old enough to be your father if I'd been, say, a little precocious in my youth.'

'If you say anything more about your age, I warn you, I'll scream and frighten the horses!'

His smile was so attractive, she thought. How could anyone say he was wild and untrustworthy? He put one arm around her and lifted her chin with his other hand so that she was encircled in an intimate grasp that was gentler but far more exciting than the bearlike fumbling embraces she had experienced from her young boy-friends.

'You're a sweet thing, Emma. I'm very tempted by the idea of an evening with you. But will your family approve?'

'Why not? My uncle likes you.'

'Extraordinary but true. He's a good chap, old Mac. And your mother?'

'She's happy as long as I am.'

And that was almost true, she hoped. 'And my reward for taking Cinderella to the ball?'

Emma knew he was teasing her, but she was only aware of the breathless excitement she felt at the warm grasp of his arm on her shoulder and the feel of those long sensitive fingers beneath her chin.

'A kiss?' she suggested.

That was what all her boy-friends wanted. They pleaded for kisses, but Emma was careful of her favours. She did not give kisses lightly and indeed had often been accused of being cold. Frankly she had never enjoyed that part of the evenings she had spent with young men. They seemed to attach an undue importance to it. But what would it be like to be kissed by a man like Jared? Her shaking heart told her it would be completely different.

'A kiss it is, then. But I must demand payment in advance.'

'Now?' she asked, startled.

'Now,' he said, his eyes laughing, close to hers.

She put her hand up to his cheek and softly kissed his mouth that was so firm against her own. He sat for a few seconds feeling the soft curve of her mouth and the moth-like touch of her hand on his face, then took his mouth away and looked down into her eyes.

'Oh, God, Emma, have you never kissed a man before?'

He gave her no time to answer before she was swept into a kiss that was as different from the one she had given him as the deer is from the tiger. She felt her lips part under his and she was drowning in throbbing waves of sweet strange desire. At last he released her, but she leaned against him and slid her hands around his bronzed shoulders.

Oh, Jared, Jared, I have been kissed before, but never like this, she thought. She put her face against his, feeling overwhelmed with happiness. He too must have felt this ecstasy, she was sure. But he firmly took her hands away and strode over to the bank of the stream.

'Where are you going?' she asked.

'Away from temptation,' he said, and turned to wave before he caught his horse by the bridle.

'But the party!' she cried, seizing upon an excuse to

17

keep him there. 'You haven't said . . . .'

'Oh, yes, the party. I'll call for you at eight. Will that do?'

'Yes, oh, yes, but Jared . . . .'

She could not bear to let him go and ran to where he was standing with the horse, two of a kind, handsome, dark and both a little frightening seen as close as this.

She had meant to say, 'Kiss me again,' but now she found she could not.

'You'll enjoy the dance, I promise you,' she said.

'I'm sure I shall,' he replied, and then he had swung his leg over the horse's back and was splashing across the river.

She had a week to think about it, a week to dream as only a romantically-minded young girl can. In her dreams Jared, in spite of all warning, became the pinnacle of all her desires, the perfect lover, the man with whom she wanted to spend her life. She went on a shopping expedition to the nearest town and drove her poor mother nearly crazy by wanting to buy slinky sophisticated garments totally unsuitable for a dance at a farm. They finally compromised by buying a pretty cotton of dark green sprigged with small white flowers, flounced at the ankles and cut in Empire style with a sash that tied high above the waist and pressed her breasts upwards so that the creamy curves showed above the heart-shaped neckline.

She began to get ready hours before the time Jared was expected. Yes, in this very bathroom, she had gone through all the rituals of bathing in scented water, polishing each nail with a rosy varnish, and arranging her hair ten times over until at last she gathered the flame-gold strands into a small pincushion of a bun on the top of her head, though silky tendrils still escaped and curled around her pale eager face.

When he came, she was desperately anxious to please

him and yet felt tonguetied, even jealous of the charm of her own mother as she chatted easily to Jared before they left. In the car she sat close to him gazing adoringly at his profile, dark in the glimmer of the dashboard lights. At last he took her hand and again she felt that quivering thrill that she had known before.

'Pretty one,' he said, and kissed the small slender fingers that were like a trembling bird in his grasp. 'You look delightful, Emma. I like the dress. It's charming, and very alluring too.'

She had half hoped, half feared he would stop the car and kiss her, but he drove straight to their destination and delivered her on to the well lit patio before going off to park. Straight away they were plunged into the gaiety of the party. The huge barn had been cleared for dancing and bales of hay arranged in a square to serve as seats.

Emma had thought that Jared would want to dance with her all evening, but it did not work out that way. He cheerfully relinquished her to the younger men who flocked around her, much to her annoyance, and he came to reclaim her at what seemed very long intervals. On one occasion an older man a little the worse for drink leered at them, remarking, 'Nothing like catching them young and training them, is there, Jared?' and another one remarked, 'Didn't know you went in for baby-snatching, old man.'

She flushed with annoyance.

'Why do they say things like that?'

'I told you, my dear, I'm way out of your age group.'

Jared laughed. He didn't even seem to care about the remarks. Emma felt his arm come around her, holding her a little more tightly, and she wished desperately that they could be alone, away from the crowd of shouting, laughing people, away from the loud jangling music and the stamp of feet that was raising the dust three feet high above the floor.

'Jared, let's go outside and walk in the garden. I want to be somewhere quiet.'

His black wings of eyebrows lifted and she felt the impact of his dark gaze.

'No, Emma.'

'Why not?' she pouted.

'Because ... because ... I'm scared of night adders.'

'Don't be so mean! I can't imagine that anything scares you.'

'Oh, yes, it does,' he assured her.

'What, then?'

'Being alone with a redhead who is sixteen and very lovely.'

'Do come,' she pleaded. 'I only want a little peace from the noisy band.'

But it was not peace she wanted. She got her way and they walked across the lawn to where spreading oaks were strung with coloured lights. There were other people in the garden, shadowy couples who wandered like wraiths in the blue night entwined in each other's embrace, not caring for anyone else but themselves. Now that they were here, to Emma the music and far-off laughter was part of the enchantment of the magic evening. He had put his arm around her to guide her over the rough grass under the trees, and now she stopped and slipped her hands around his neck.

'Are you glad you came?' she asked.

'Very glad, my sweet one.'

'Am I your sweet one, am I really, Jared?'

He did not answer but put his arms around her, responding to the feel of warm young hands on his skin, the whole fragrant allure of Emma, young, vibrant, eager for his caresses.

His mouth came down upon hers, gently at first, and then with a savage insistence. When he released her she almost fell and far above her in the velvet depths of the

African night, the blazing stars spun in dizzying glory. He held her close, steadying her trembling body against his, and she clung to him, feeling the hard maleness of him against her, and wanting nothing else but that he should go on kissing her, making love to her, until they were both caught up in passion as ageless and glorious as the stars.

From the lighted barn came the sound of a waltz followed by the strains of Auld Lang Syne, laughter and cheering.

'It's over, Emma. We must go. We should say good-bye to our hostess.'

What had she looked like as she entered the lighted room? Her hair had been descending in curling shining locks and she felt incandescent as if a flame had been lit inside her. She said her farewells in a dream and she noticed that people looked at her oddly, but she did not care. All she knew was that she would be in Jared's company for the long drive home. But this was not to be. She would never know whether her hostess, the mother of a girl as young as herself, had noticed her appearance and put two and two together, but she noticed her speak to Jared and two people detached themselves from a group and came towards them.

'So kind of you to say you can give us a lift. Sure it won't be out of your way?'

Jared smiled charmingly.

'Not at all. I'll drop Emma first and then take you on to your place.'

'Oh, but . . .!' Emma began.

But what could she say? I thought I was going to be alone with you. I wanted more of your kisses. I thought we would discuss what's to be done if we're both in love. She swallowed her disappointment, although it was bitter, and told herself that now she and Jared had found each other they would have a whole lifetime to be together. What did it matter if they were to be parted for

21

a few hours? She had to be satisfied with the brief kiss he gave her in the presence of the others and then she was alone, but alone to dream of the evening, to think of every word he said, every caress they had shared.

In spite of the late night, she was up early next day, waiting for the phone call that she was sure would come. When ten o'clock had passed and there was still no message from him, she could contain her impatience no longer and decided to ride down to the stream where they had met before. Of course he would not phone. How foolish of her to think he would! The farm phones were on party lines and anyone lifting their receiver would be able to hear everything they said. Either he would call to see her or expect to meet her while out riding. She took care to tell the servants where she was going so that he would know if he came to the house.

She sat beside the stream, smelling again the hot fragrance of the wild grasses and remembering their first kiss. What would happen? There were only three weeks left before she was due to go back to England with her mother. But she could not go back now. She was certain that Jared felt as she did and that he would want to marry her as soon as possible. People would say she was young, but she was old for her age and those ancestors of hers in the dining-room, staid as they looked, had married in their teens when they were early settlers in this country.

She closed her eyes and willed him to appear. 'Jared, Jared, I'm waiting for you. Do please come.' But nothing happened, and though she waited for another hour she saw no sign of him and there was no message when she got back to the house. Desperate now, she decided she would ride over to Heron's Creek that afternoon. Something must have happened to him, or otherwise why had he not got in touch with her after the romantic emotions they had shared last night?

She had never been to Heron's Creek before, but she

knew the way, for she had often ridden in that direction and seen the large sprawling house with its rose red bricks and its numerous matching outbuildings. Jacaranda trees, standing in their own reflections of fallen purple blossom made an avenue to the front door and there were clumps of blue gum trees with their curious peeling silver bark. The roof was of weathered tiles, mossy and old, where grey doves, their plumage iridescent in the sunlight, paraded upon it with sure pink feet.

Emma drew her horse to a halt beneath the purple shade of a jacaranda tree murmurous with the sound of bees, and looked at the house. Where would Jared be at this time in the afternoon? How was she to find him? The heavy door was open and a golden labrador lay in the porch beside the curious stone figures that stared out from the sides of the steps.

Whose was the car drawn up near the house? Could it be Jared's? Or was it a visitor's? It was a small sports car, certainly not the one he had used last night – but then he would hardly have used it to take her to a dance. She knew so little about him, but, she assured herself, that would soon be remedied. She knew everything that was of importance, she thought, the fact that they loved each other.

As she hesitated, she saw two figures come to the door; one was the tall lean one that she felt she knew so well, Jared, casually dressed in jeans and a thin shirt open to the waist, and the other was a woman, her hair glinting silver blonde in the sunlight, wearing a gay skirt and a halter top tied beneath her breasts so that her beautiful brown back and waist were bare. They had not noticed her beneath the dark shade of the jacaranda, and yet in the clear still afternoon air she could hear their conversation.

'I hate to leave you, Jared, after our lovely afternoon, but I'll have to go now. David is always so frightfully suspicious if I'm late home these days.'

'That's risky, Elvira. I told you before you shouldn't come over here so often.'

The blonde woman laughed with a husky, exciting note.

'Try to stop me, Jared, you devil, after an afternoon like this one!'

She put her arms around him and they kissed in a long embrace until Emma felt she wanted to scream. At last the woman turned to go to the car.

'Good-bye, my love, I must fly. I don't know how I'll survive without you.'

The car roared down the drive and Jared turned to go indoors, but Emma had urged on her horse, trotted to the front steps and slid down to greet him. Jared frowned, his eyes dark with displeasure. It was not all the kind of greeting she had imagined in her lovely dreams.

'Emma, what in heaven's name are you doing here?'

Emma hurled herself up the steps, her red hair flying loose behind her, her eyes stormy.

'Who was she? What was she doing here?'

Jared looked at her angry face and laughed. She wanted to hit him, to strike the curving firm mouth that she so loved.

'What's it got to do with you, Emma, I should like to know?'

'I thought it had everything to do with me. Who is she? Do you love her better than me?'

She was beside herself with rage and jealousy. Just as before she had never known she could feel such physical passion for a man, now she did not know how to deal with these angry emotions that were spoiling her dreams of love.

He put his hands on her shoulders and drew her into the house. In spite of her anger she felt thrilled by his touch.

'Emma, what is this? If you intend to make a scene, you'd better come inside.'

A bright fire glowed in the stone fireplace and a comfortable settee was drawn up in front of it. In the air she could detect a faint ghost of French perfume. Was this where he and that woman had spent their lovely afternoon? She burst into tears of rage at the picture her mind conjured up of Jared and the blonde woman locked in a warm embrace, the husky voice whispering intimately as he caressed that brown beautiful body. Jared took her by the shoulders and shook her anything but gently.

'Stop this nonsense at once, Emma! If there's one thing I can't stand, it's an hysterical woman. What possessed you to come here, and why are you crying?'

'I'm not,' Emma denied hotly, gulping down her tears and furiously wiping her eyes. 'I've been waiting all day for you to phone or come to see me. I thought something had happened to you, so I came here – and then I saw you with this woman. Who is she?'

'A friend,' Jared answered. He spoke coldly and Emma found his expression frightening, but she had to know more.

'What did she come for?'

She had just had a wild idea that he might have sent for this other woman to tell her everything was over between them because now he had found the love of his life, but then she remembered the conversation she had heard and it seemed hardly likely.

'She came to say good-bye to me.' Emma smiled through her tears. So it was true. He had been sending her away. Maybe she had misunderstood what she had heard. Jared had drawn her upon the couch and now she flung her arms around him.

'Oh, Jared darling, I'm sorry I was cross. I didn't understand. You mean you've told her about us?'

'About us? What on earth are you talking about, Emma? She's never even met you. She came to say good-bye to me because I won't be seeing her for a while – I'm leaving on a game-fishing trip tomorrow to the Comorro Islands. I expect to be away at least six weeks.'

Emma dropped her arms and raised stricken eyes to look at him. How could he look so calm when he had just given her a blow to the heart that made her feel as if she were facing death itself?

'But . . . six weeks! You can't go away now, Jared. We leave to go back to London in three weeks' time.'

His expression was gentler now and he put his arm around her shoulder. She leaned against him feeling weak with despair.

'I know, my dear, but on the whole I think it's all for the best, don't you agree?'

'For the best? Jared, how can you say that? Do you really mean that it's for the best that we never meet again?'

He gave her a little shake.

'Emma, don't make such a big drama of it. We've only met three times for very brief periods. You can't have dreamed up a big romance from such a small thing.'

She was cut to the heart.

'A small thing? Is that all last night meant to you, Jared, and that time when you kissed me down by the river, was that just a small thing to you?'

He sighed rather wearily, and that, more than anything that had gone before, made her realize that he, anything but a patient man, was trying to deal with her gently.

'Of course, Emma, it was delightful. I enjoyed our brief encounter by the river more than I can say, and as for last night, it was charming of you to ask me to the party. I've seldom enjoyed an evening more.'

'But . . . but. . . .'

Oh, how could she get through to him, how convey that what had been a delightful evening to him had been

26

an earth-shaking event to her?

'But I thought,' she said, knowing desperately that she sounded naïve but not knowing how to stop herself, 'I thought if two people felt as we did last night in the garden that it would be ... well, that it would make us both very happy if we married each other.'

'Oh, Emma, my child, you're young, but not so ignorant as to think that a few kisses, a few embraces, and I admit they were very lovely, could constitute a basis for spending one's life together.'

She stared at him, white-faced, all her dreams in the dust, feeling nothing but shame that she had behaved as she had with him and he had felt none of the ecstasy she had imagined.

'I suppose I'm no gentleman to remind you of it, Emma,' he went on, 'but it was at your wish that we went into the garden, wasn't it? Neither am I a saint when a pretty girl shows she's eager to be kissed. As for marriage, even if I wanted to marry, you must know it's common gossip that my affairs are in a hopeless tangle. I'm thinking of selling the farm and going to Australia to start a new life.'

'And you don't want me to have any part in that life?' asked Emma slowly.

'Emma, believe me, if I'd known how you would feel I would never have taken you to the dance, but for God's sake, just because you take a teenager to a party and give her a few kisses ... one would think I'd seduced you!'

'I wish you had,' said Emma sadly. 'I might have had some claim on you then.'

She rose to go, for she felt she could not stand seeing him any more, the man she thought she had loved with all her heart.

'Don't hate me too much. You'll forget me in a couple of days,' Jared assured her. 'When you get back to London, you'll meet someone your own age, and if you do

27

remember me you'll laugh to think of it.'

But she never had. She remembered that the next day a box of a dozen long-stemmed red roses arrived at the farm from a town florist with message, 'Roses for a rose of a girl.' There was nothing more. She supposed Jared could not say anything else for fear her mother might see it. For months she had hated herself more than him because she felt she had cheapened herself by her ardent response to his experienced lovemaking, and that it had meant nothing to him. She had been very cautious with other men she had met, but actually she had not needed to be. There was not any need to restrain herself, for never again had she felt the physical response she had sensed with Jared, the dark stranger who could have taken her so easily.

She was grown up now. The hurt and foolishness were buried beneath five years of living, but perhaps it had done her good to think it over. Now she could feel free of it on her first night back at Sunglow. And Jared? Her uncle had mentioned once that he had gone to Australia. He had not spoken of him again, but then his letters were always infrequent and had stopped altogether during the last year. Emma had been surprised and overjoyed that he had left the farm to her. There would be other problems, she supposed, more practical than the ones she had had to face here before.

She got out of the bath and started to dry herself on the fluffy primrose towel. The water was gushing out of the yellow bath and the noise was so great that she had not heard anything else, so she was enormously startled by someone knocking on the door of the bathroom. It must be Rosie, the maid. Perhaps she had returned to the house and discovered she was there. She wrapped the towel around her, calling, 'I'm coming, Rosie!' and opened the door.

But it was not the old African servant she had known so well. In khaki jeans with a blue shirt open showing the bronze of his chest, Jared stood before her, his black hair curling away from his brows, his winglike eyebrows black against the dark expressive eyes.

'Who's in there?' he had just shouted, but as she opened the door, he stepped back and his eyes widened. 'What the hell are you doing here, Emma?'

'I could say the same to you, Jared,' she answered sharply. 'What gives you the right to come crashing into my bathroom like this?'

And into my life again, she thought with panic, as she wrapped the towel more firmly around her.

'It happens to be my bathroom too,' said Jared. 'I'm living here, didn't anyone tell you?'

CHAPTER TWO

'You can't be!' Emma gasped. 'How can you be living here? The farm has been left to me.'

'Of course, I know that. I'll explain later. Delightful as you look wrapped in that towel, I think I'd better let you get some clothes on. I was going to get Rosie to scramble some eggs. Will that do for you?'

'Yes,' Emma nodded.

He strode out of the bedroom and she was left to pat herself dry and ruefully look at herself in the mirror. She was very flushed, and her hair was standing up in wild wisps of curls in an aureole around her small head. If she had ever dreamed of meeting Jared again it was as a svelte, sophisticated, grown-up person, not the tousled sight that greeted her in her own reflection. She tried to remedy things by clean clothes and brushed her hair until it took some kind of neat shape swirled around her head. She used a little make-up, some coloured foundation and a coral lipstick. There, that was better. The brown top clung to the curves of her breasts. She tied a green scarf around her neck and knotted it loosely. Why was she taking this trouble? She would not have used make-up or added the scarf if she had been supping alone.

Whatever was Jared doing here? How could he be living at this farm, her farm, when he should be living over at Heron's Creek? She would soon know. One thing was certain – her hopes of a peaceful evening dreaming of her happy future life here were shattered. Imagine having to have supper with Jared on her very first night at the farm! But she was no longer a teenager, she assured herself. She was well able to cope with any situation, however unwelcome and awkward.

Her chin was determined, her dark blue eyes the colour of a summer storm, as she marched along the passage and down the stairs. Someone – it must have been Jared – had put a match to the log fire that was set in the stone fireplace. A few lamps had been lit, but there was a pool of darkness where Jared stood, leaning in a negligent attitude, his elbow on the mantel, his dark profile outlined by the reflection of the leaping flames, a glass in his hands.

Emma was instantly annoyed by the air of possession about him. How dare he look as if he owned the place? He glanced up as she entered and came towards her.

'Ah, Emma, now I can greet you properly. Sorry I barged in like that. I don't know which of us can have been the more surprised.'

He put his hands on her shoulders and drew her towards the light.

'Little Emma, quite grown-up now, and still very lovely, but with lavender shadows under those dark blue eyes. Are you very tired after your journey? What will you drink? Whisky or brandy? I don't keep anything else here, except beer, and I hardly think you need that.'

He had put his own glass on the table and now drew her towards the couch with its soft springbok kaross.

'Sit down, Emma. I think whisky would do you good.'

She sat and accepted the drink he offered, though inwardly she was seething at the way he was playing host to her in her own house. But she was even more alarmed by the fact that at his touch she had felt a quivering thrill that she was totally unaccustomed to feel when she met other men. It's my imagination, she told herself. It's because he was the first man who kissed me so that I felt a passionate attraction. But he means nothing to me now – and I don't intend that he should.

'Now perhaps you would be good enough to explain to me what you're doing here,' she said crisply.

He grinned. No man had any right to have such a winning smile, she thought.

'Emma, my love, you must know you're beautiful. No one who looks as lovely as you should sound like an old-fashioned schoolmarm!'

'I'm not sixteen any more, Jared. There's no need for flattery. It won't make any impression on me, I assure you. I'm asking you a simple question: why are you staying here?'

He smiled ruefully and went to refill his glass.

'I can see I'm not going to be very popular around here – I wonder why? If I remember correctly we got on together quite well when we met before.'

How could he be so brash? Surely he could not think they had parted good friends, but maybe he did not even remember the details of their few meetings? Certainly it had meant very little to him.

'I'm waiting for your explanation,' she informed him coldly.

'Oh, that . . .!' He tilted his glass and admired the colour of the whisky reflected in the firelight. 'This is almost the colour of your hair, Emma. Thank God that hasn't changed even if you have.'

'How have I changed?' she could not resist asking.

'If I remember correctly you were a sweet alluring child, impetuous and full of charm.'

'And now?'

'Now . . .' his smile was teasing. How well she remembered it! 'I'm not saying anything. First impressions aren't always correct. We'll have plenty of time to get to know each other better.'

'What do you mean? Why should we get to know each other better?'

'My dear Emma, I've been managing the farm for the last year since old Mac fell ill and wasn't able to do as much. He offered me the job and I was glad to take it. I'd

32

let my own farm to some Australians I'd met while I was out there.'

'Then you did go to Australia?'

She was sorry she had said this. It showed she had taken an interest in his life.

'Yes, I did, for three years. How did you know? I tried to settle there, but I missed my own country too much. I hadn't sold the farm, so I came back, but my affairs were in a tangle from my misspent youth and when I had an opportunity to let the farm to my rich Australian friends, I seized it in order to recoup my losses for a while.'

'And to work for my Uncle Mac? But things will be different now, Jared. I fully intend to run this farm on my own. I won't need a manager.'

'Won't you now? Don't be too sure, Emma.'

If you were the last man in the world, she thought, I wouldn't have you working for me here. Certainly I don't want to have anything to do with you in my new life.

But she did not say it aloud. She could wait until she had seen Mr. Johnson, her attorney, and had the position explained to her.

'Let's not argue about it now,' said Jared, as if he had been reading her thoughts. 'I don't often have the company of a pretty girl for supper. I must make the most of it, mustn't I?'

'I can hardly believe that,' said Emma.

'Oh, yes, I'm a reformed character these days,' he assured her.

'Are you married, then?' asked Emma. Nothing would surprise her, she thought.

'God forbid! I have no ambitions in that direction. And you, Emma? Married – engaged?'

'I have no ambitions in that direction either, Jared.'

So you are quite safe, she wanted to add.

He refilled her glass without being asked and now came to sit beside her. The leaping flames emphasized the warm colour of her hair and the half light enhanced the deep blue of her eyes. She was conscious of his dark eyes examining her curiously.

'You were a lovely teenager, Emma,' he said, 'but now you're a beautiful woman — and that's not flattery. I wonder how you've managed to stay single until now.'

'I've remained heartfree,' she said. Because of you, she could have added. Having your heart bruised at sixteen is a lesson you don't easily forget.

'And yet many men must have been attracted to you.'

'Oh, yes, yes, yes, I have to fight them off in hordes.'

She had not meant to laugh with him, and yet here they were both smiling at each other. His long slender fingers briefly caressed her own.

'That's better. Now you've forgotten to be stern. Here's Rosie with the food trolley. I told her to bring it in here. I didn't think you would want to eat in the dining-room on your first night here.'

He had taken everything out of her hands, she thought, but she got up to meet the old African maid, who greeted her with laughter, a few tears, loud exclamations and even a prayer of thanks for her safe arrival.

It was too intimate, Emma thought, as they sat beside the fire with trays on their laps. She wished she did not feel so conscious of this man's presence. And yet that brief touch of his hand had sent a flame coursing through her body. It was nothing but physical magnetism, she assured herself, and he possessed it in an extreme way. She could not tolerate the idea of seeing him every day when he had this effect on her. Tomorrow she must find out how she could get rid of him.

When they had finished eating and Rosie had said good night and gone to her own quarters, the house seemed very quiet. Emma was conscious now that they were alone in an isolation that she had not experienced since leaving Africa five years ago. In the garden, the crickets kept up their continual piercing chorus, but there were no customary sounds, no noise of traffic, no radios from other people's flats. With the exception of the servants far away from the house in their own rooms, there was probably not another person within a distance of miles.

The unaccustomed whisky, the meal, the warmth of the fire and the comfort of the old-fashioned deeply soft couch was making her physically drowsy, and yet her mind was wide awake, thinking over the strange situation in which she had found herself.

'I hardly expected to find you here,' she said.

'Nor I you.'

Jared stretched and she was conscious of his body like that of a lithe, spirited animal.

'Frankly, I did not expect you would come back,' he went on, 'nor, I think, did Mr. Johnson who's dealing with the estate. He hardly thought this life would appeal to a girl from London. He was going to suggest he should put the farm up for sale.'

'I realized he didn't get my letter, telling him of my intentions, but anyhow I'll see him tomorrow and find out all about it – but, Jared, I warn you I'm quite serious when I say I want to run it on my own.'

'Don't let's argue so late in the evening. I'll show you around the place tomorrow, but first I'll take you to see Mr. Johnson. We'll see what you have to say after that.'

He looked at her with a dark gleam of laughter in his eyes.

'Why are you smiling?' asked Emma. 'Is there something you know that I don't?'

'Wait and see,' he said.

He put his arm around her, enclosing her shoulders in that gentle charming embrace that she remembered so well, and now his long slender fingers had taken her face to turn it towards him.

'Let me look at you, Emma. Yes, you are lovely, but

not, I think, suitable to be a farmer.'

She shrugged furiously away from him, her eyes stormy, her red hair glinting in the firelight as she swung herself up from the couch.

'You know nothing whatsoever about me, Jared. You never have. And if you're used to women who like your casual lovemaking, I'm not one of them!'

He had risen and was smiling down at her, his eyes dark in the half light of the shadowed room.

'Lovemaking . . . hardly that, surely? I don't remember such virtuous indignation when we met before. Emma, Emma, it's very natural for a man to admire a beautiful woman.'

'But not to touch her, Jared, against her wishes. Please remember that. When we met before I was very young and very impressionable, but that doesn't apply any more.'

He shrugged his shoulders.

'As you wish. You've certainly changed. But I'll remember my place in future. You are of course the mistress here.' He grinned wickedly. 'My mistress.'

'But not for long, Jared,' Emma said coldly, ignoring the innuendo. How infuriating he was! She felt she could not stand another moment of it. But she was even more angry with herself, for she realized with shame that her body longed for his touch, that she still had the same feelings towards him that she had had as a teenager, even though she no longer thought of him almost as a god. Oh, how could her physical self betray her so, when her sensible mind disliked this man so completely?

'If you'll be kind enough to tell me where I can sleep,' she said caustically, 'I'll go to bed now.'

'I presume the room with the yellow roses was yours, and it still is. Rosie always keeps the beds made up and aired.'

She hesitated, wanting to ask him where he was sleeping. Finally she said, 'And you?'

'My dear virtuous spinster, I have the interleading room. Any objections?'

She wanted to hit the sardonic curve of his mouth.

'Yes, I have. I want that apartment to myself. Is there nowhere else where you can sleep?'

He put his hand across his chest and bowed towards her. 'Madam's every wish is a command. I'll take myself as far away from her as possible. Old Mac used to keep a camp bed in his museum in the outbuilding across the yard. I'll take a blanket and sleep there and your reputation will be secure, we hope, but tell me who's to know if I sleep there or in the house?'

'I don't care who knows,' declined Emma. 'I just don't want you in the house.'

'I'm hurt now,' said Jared. 'Emma darling, you don't trust me.'

'No, I don't,' said Emma. 'Good night, Jared.'

'What? Not even a kiss? And I am to be banished to the museum amongst all the ghosties and long leggity beasties? What a tyrant I have for a mistress!'

She turned her back on him, trying to hide a smile.

'Come, then, if I'm to be dismissed like this you'd better lock me out,' said Jared. 'Rosie has the back door key. You must lock the front one.'

Had she been over-cautious, she thought, as she lay in bed unable to sleep in spite of her weariness? Was it really old-maidish not to want him to sleep in the same house? He was older than her in years and experience and possibly he found her reactions ridiculous, but she was determined not to take a chance. No, she reflected, it was not altogether that she mistrusted him, but it was herself of whom she was afraid. Oh, well, tomorrow she would sort out the situation, she promised herself as she tossed and turned upon the bed that had foot and headboard made of white painted wickerwork. She had slept for many hours in this bed worn out by a day's activity, tennis, riding, swimming, dancing, with never a single worry until Jared came along. And now here he was causing her worry again.

She tried to lie still now and compose her mind to sleep, but again she became conscious of the silence of the dark African night, and now she was alone it began to oppress her. When she listened it was not exactly silent. A long way off there was the eerie shriek of an owl, and a plover called from the farmlands, sounding lonely and forlorn. Somewhere, perhaps at Heron's Creek, a dog howled to the moon. Emma began to wish she had not been so hasty in dismissing Jared. It would have been good to feel he was sleeping somewhere nearby. The old museum building was right across the yard. Why had she let him go? It had been all nonsense thinking that she had still felt this wild attraction. It was because of the shock of seeing him again and because she was tired from the journey and more susceptible. She was used to looking after herself and had nothing to fear, but all the same this first night alone here was a bit intimidating.

What was that? Distinctly she heard footsteps upon the patio below her window. Heart beating wildly, she went to the window. Someone was there. She saw the flash of a torch, swiftly concealed.

'Who's there?' she called firmly. 'Don't come any further. I have a gun!'

'Good God, Emma,' said Jared's voice, 'are you going to shoot me now? I came to see if I could get in some way to find a fresh supply of tobacco. That bed's damn hard and I need some consolation. Sorry I startled you.'

'I'll let you in,' said Emma, and hastily put on her pale green dressing gown. It was one that her mother had passed on to her and was a little too fluffy for her simpler taste, with an edging of soft marabou feathers in the same eau-de-nil green and a sash that tied underneath her breasts. Jared's eyes widened as she opened the door.

'Well, it was worth losing sleep for such a lovely vision, wasn't it?'

Why did he make her feel instantly on the defensive?

'I'm losing sleep, too, Jared. Would you please get your tobacco and go.'

He shook his head. 'How can she be so lovely and speak so cruelly?' he asked of no one in particular.

'Can you really not sleep in that bed?' she asked.

'Come across and see it. I'd like you to know what you've condemned me to.'

She looked at him suspiciously.

'Don't look at me like that. Truly, Emma, I haven't an evil intention in my head.'

'I'll come tomorrow morning,' she promised.

'And leave me all night in dire distress? You don't think of the comfort of your employees, Emma. I'm surprised at you!'

'Oh, all right, I'll come.'

He could always get his own way, she thought, that was the trouble. What was she doing, acting against her better judgment, walking across to the outbuilding, his arm around her guiding her, the grass wet to her bare feet, and the warm wind bringing with it the scent of blossom, heady and intoxicating? She was reminded of that night long ago when she was sixteen and they had walked in the garden underneath the oaks.

She tried to pull herself together and told herself she was just going to see the room to which she had banished him and decide whether he was exaggerating about its discomfort, but feeling his hand at her waist, knowing they were alone in this moonlit silver night, with the warm perfume of an African spring in the air, she mistrusted him, and most of all herself.

'I can find my way across the grass without your help,' she said to him, attempting to remove his arm.

39

'I feel responsible for your safety,' Jared explained. 'I have brought you out here, after all. It's only common sense for me to guide you. What a standoffish person you've become, Emma!'

'I'm not standoffish,' she denied indignantly. Why could he always put her in the wrong? 'But I don't like men thinking they can casually caress me when it doesn't mean a thing to them.'

'For heaven's sake, you certainly want a man to be a knight in shining armour to suit you, don't you, Emma? I didn't realize it was such an honour to touch you – in fact I thought I was being courteous in helping you over the rough ground. But if that's how you feel, you can find your own way.'

He dropped his arm and instantly she was sorry. In spite of herself she had felt thrilled by this intimate contact with him. It hadn't meant anything to him, obviously, so why had she been such a fool as to make a fuss about it?

'Here we are,' he said, and opened the door of the museum.

It certainly was very eerie at this time of night, illuminated by two or three dim lamps, the vast barnlike building stretched up to the dark ceiling above. There were cases filled with animal skulls and skeletons, bottles filled with liquid in which dead snakes reposed, large heads of animals on the walls, antelope, a leopard, a lion, a snarling hyena, a collection of old pistols. It might have been interesting during the day, but at night it looked weird and repulsive. On the dusty bare floor there was a camp bed, rather old and broken down, covered by a rumpled blanket.

Emma gave a shudder. 'I can see what you mean, now,' she said. 'You'd better come back into the house, Jared.'

After all, she thought to herself, it's only for a little

40

while, just until I can get things sorted out and make more suitable arrangements.

'Aren't you kind?' said Jared. 'And not before time, if I may say so.'

Perhaps she had been hard on him. It was foolish to bear a grudge for five years. She was going to make a new life here for herself, but she had not planned that any man should have a part in it.

Jared's flattering speeches were all part and parcel of his make-up. He had obviously been used to being sought by women for so many years that now he was just doing it to her from force of habit, as he had done when she was sixteen and had thrown herself at his head. Well, there would not be any more of that this time.

They walked back to the house a little apart from each other. She missed his guiding arm, but she could hardly expect it after the objections she had raised.

'We'll go to the kitchen and make a hot drink so that you can sleep for the rest of the night, Emma,' Jared told her. He doesn't ask whether I want it, she thought, but really it seemed a good idea. The fire in the stove was still glowing with hot wood ash and Jared added some fuel and helped himself to milk from the pantry. Emma sat on a wooden chair, raising her feet on to the rung to keep them off the cold floor.

'Why haven't you got any shoes on, Emma, you foolish girl? Your feet must be frozen from all that dew.'

'They are a bit cold and wet,' Emma admitted. 'And this stupid dressing gown is wet all around the hem.'

'Take it off, then,' he advised her. 'You won't be cold by the stove. Here, let me dry your feet.'

He slipped off the fluffy negligée and proceeded to towel her feet dry. She was very conscious that she was clad only in a flimsy nightdress of diaphanous pale green voile, but could not find the courage to protest after all the previous argument. He looked at her briefly.

41

'Here, take my jacket,' he said.

He slipped her arms into the sleeves, feeling the warmth from his body and smelling the smoky fragrance of tobacco combined with something else ... sandalwood? After-shave cologne? Anyhow, it was pleasant, she decided. Jared was still on his knees drying her feet.

'I can do that,' she protested.

'But you won't do it as well as me,' he told her. 'Here, put your feet on the rug and I'll make our hot drinks.'

'I didn't know you could be so domesticated,' she commented.

'Years of living on my own and expeditions into the bush have made me capable of a little domestication, if you could call it that ... frying an egg, making an omelette, grilling a steak.'

'Haven't you ever felt the need of a wife?' she asked.

He sighed with exasperation and handed her the frothy chocolate.

'You disappoint me, Emma. Wherever I've lived, every woman in the neighbourhood has tried to get me married to someone. Women seem to think there's something disgraceful about a single man. It puts them on their mettle.'

'But ... but ... there are other things to marriage besides acquiring a cook and housekeeper,' she protested.

He grinned, the dark eyebrows raised in black wings above the dazzling light of his laughing eyes.

'There are indeed, Emma, but I've found my pleasures elsewhere. Attractive women, Emma, are mostly passionate and unfaithful, and who am I to deny this delightful fact?'

'You don't seem to have much opinion of women.'

'I've no objection to them. To paraphrase that cigarette advert – some of my best friends are women. But my standards are high. Find me one who's beautiful and prepared to love me and charm me for the whole of my life and maybe I might even consider marriage. Oh, and I almost forgot, she must have money too, and never, never look at any other man.'

'What will she get in return for all this?' asked Emma.

'Me,' answered Jared, smiling. 'That should be enough, don't you agree?'

'No, I don't, but then this is all purely theoretical, for you'll never find this perfect woman who's going to adore you – you're far too exasperating, Jared.'

You should have married me when I was sixteen, she thought, too young to know better.

'Whatever makes you think I'm exasperating?' asked Jared. 'I'm very normal and good-tempered, placid as all get out. Maybe I should try to find some nice meek little woman to match me.'

'Placid?' exclaimed Emma. 'You certainly don't give me that impression.'

'I'm a bit allergic to redheads who are used to getting their own way. So you needn't be alarmed, Emma, for you don't fit into the picture of my meek little hand-maiden of a wife.'

'I should hope I don't,' said Emma. 'And now I'm going to bed.'

She knew he was teasing her, and yet his careless dismissal of her as a redhead who was used to getting her own way had hurt. How foolish of her to feel this! She stood up.

'Here's your jacket,' she said.

She felt that Jared's eyes were on her.

'All the same,' he said, 'this particular redhead looks very delectable in pale green. Aren't I fortunate to have such a lovely mistress – sorry, employer? Good night, Emma. Sleep well, and don't worry to lock your door. I'm quite trustworthy as far as you're concerned. I know when I'm not wanted.'

Did he? she thought, lying awake for a while longer, but not hearing him come up the stairs. At least now she knew she had managed to conceal her stupid reactions from him. How could she possibly feel such physical attraction to a man like Jared who was, in spite of what he had said, everything she mistrusted? This poor meek wife he spoke of acquiring would never have a moment's peace. He had lived according to his own whims and desires for far too long to be a satisfactory partner to anyone. But why had she started thinking of marriage? That had nothing to do with her problem, which was that he considered he was the farm's manager and that she must find how she could send him away – and the further the better.

CHAPTER THREE

'I've gone to the lands, but shall be back later to fetch you to go to town and see Mr. Johnson. I peeped in and you looked so beautiful asleep that I gave instructions to Rosie to leave you until you woke. If you ring, she'll bring your breakfast.'

Emma had awakened refreshed and rested after some hours' sleep, but was taken aback to find the note on her pillow. She was indignant that he had come in and seen her asleep. What had she looked like, actually? She was suspicious of Jared's flattery – it was just a habit of his. She rang for Rosie who arrived with a tray laden with bacon, eggs and kidneys under a silver dome, mountains of toast and honey, and a silver jug of coffee, fragrant and strong.

Later she dressed carefully, wearing her best slacks suit of cream linen with an emerald silk knit sweater and Italian leather shoes of the same shade. She brushed out her hair until it shone like copper, waving on her shoulders, but then decided she had better look sedate to meet her attorney and drew it into a pleated knot at the back. Creamy make-up and apricot lipstick completed her appearance. She had not expected to have to dress up so soon. She had visualized herself on the first morning putting on an old pair of jeans and a shirt and doing a tour of the farm. But that could come later, she hoped.

'*Hau! Inhle!* Miss Emma looks beautiful. Where you go?' exclaimed Rosie when she saw her.

'To the town, Rosie. I have to see Mr. Johnson.'

'*Hau*, Miss Emma, it won't be long before you find a man. All of them, they will all want you looking like that!'

'I'm glad you think so, Rosie. Is there anything you

want me to bring for you from town?'

'I give the master a list of groceries. He always brings them for me.'

Jared certainly had taken over, Emma reflected. She would have to alter that, but it was no use doing anything about it now. The term 'manager' was right, for he was managing everything, inside and out. But it was early days yet.

It was a clear sunny day, not too hot, and while she was waiting for Jared Emma sat on the verandah on a wrought iron chair, one of four that were grouped around a heavy white iron table intricately worked with figures of cupids and hearts. She remembered that it had belonged to one of her earlier relatives and that her mother had retrieved it from an outside shed, dirty and neglected, and transformed it into an enviable piece of outdoor furniture.

It was a nuisance, she reflected, that she had to wait for Jared to take her into town. When she understood her financial position she must see whether it would be possible to get a little car. Meanwhile she must sit in this lovely mild sunshine and try to be calm, to compose herself for dealing with business affairs, and to stop the little quivers that afflicted her inside when she thought of another meeting with Jared.

But when she saw the small four-wheel-drive vehicle with its trail of dust along the farm road as it approached the house, her heart beat more quickly.

'Won't be long,' he shouted as he parked it in the shade. 'I must change to go into town, I suppose.'

He dashed into the house and she heard his feet pounding up the stairs. In a few minutes he was back, his black curls smooth, his olive safari suit well cut but casual. A bright patterned Liberty cravat was knotted loosely around his neck, but he still looked like a reckless pirate, she decided.

'Wow!' he exclaimed when he saw her. 'Is all this for me?'

'No, it's not. It's for Mr. Johnson. I certainly would not make any effort to dress up for your sake.'

'I think you did once,' said Jared, smiling.

How dared he remind her? She was silent, ignoring his remark completely.

'Anyhow, I'm the one who'll be in your company most, so the effort is not wasted on me,' said Jared.

He knows so well how to please a woman, thought Emma. It's very difficult to resist compliments. He knows that any woman feels wonderful if she's told she looks good. As they drove into town, she stole a glance at him every now and again. The five years that had changed her from a girl into a woman had had hardly any effect on him. His black hair sprang thickly from his unwrinkled brow, his profile was as clearcut and as handsome as it ever was, his lean frame like that of a youth, lithe and supple.

Oh, why had this man had to come back into her life, when everything else was so pleasant – the mellow sun, the blue hills, the regular rows of blossoming trees with their dark shiny evergreen leaves and here and there some late oranges still hanging unpicked upon them? She remembered the attractive little town well. It was in a valley surrounded by hills, some of them could be called mountains by English standards. The houses were white bungalows standing in their own large gardens, and in the centre of the town was a circle where there was an old war memorial surrounded by a small pretty park gay with Iceland poppies, pink, yellow, flame colour, and trees of flowing peach and plum.

'Mr. Johnson's office is in the main street,' Jared told her, 'I'll leave you there and then go to the agricultural supply place. I expect you'll be some time there. Shall we meet at the hotel for lunch?'

'Very well. But don't you want some help in buying Rosie's groceries?'

'My dear Emma, I think I know more about buying food for the Africans than you do. How long is it since you've seen mealie meal and samp, and what kind of meat would you buy for them?'

'Don't we grow our own maize?' asked Emma.

'Yes, but there's not enough at the end of the winter after having to feed the workers who pick the fruit.'

'And meat? Do we keep sheep and cattle?'

'Yes, indeed, but for breeding and wool rather than killing.'

'I'm glad of that,' said Emma.

He left her at Mr. Johnson's office and she went up the stairs of the old Victorian building. The African clerk announced her and the old attorney came hurrying out of his office to usher her in.

'My dear Miss Page, how nice to see you! This is a pleasant surprise. I wondered what on earth had happened to you. I hadn't heard a word.'

'My letters must have been affected by the strike,' said Emma, sitting down. 'I gather you weren't expecting me?'

'No, indeed, but I'm very glad to see you. Now I can explain the terms of the will more fully. I was going to give you details in writing, but now you're here I can make it clearer, for it's a bit complicated.'

Emma looked at the old man with his white hair and sideburns and his mild blue eyes. Everyone looked as if they spent a lot of time out of doors, she reflected. His cheeks were pink from the sun. She supposed he spent his leisure time on the local bowling green as most of the older men did.

'How do you mean . . . complicated?' she asked.

'Oh, not particularly difficult. Don't be alarmed. Actually it's a very sensible provision that your uncle made, in my opinion. Though of course, as I said, I wasn't expecting you would come here yourself or want to live here. But perhaps he thought you would.'

'But what is the provision?' asked Emma, trying not to sound impatient.

'Your uncle made it a condition of inheriting the farm that you keep Jared Wells as manager for a period of two years.'

'Two years? But that's impossible!' Emma exclaimed.

Mr. Johnson looked surprised. Behind his steel-rimmed spectacles, his eyes widened until, Emma thought, he looked for all the world like a fluffy white-feathered barn owl.

'What makes you say that?' he asked. 'At the time your uncle stipulated this I thought it a very sensible arrangement.'

'But . . . but I don't need a manager. I came here with the idea that I would run the farm on my own.'

Mr. Johnson looked still more amazed.

'My dear young lady, an orange farm takes a great deal of management. Do you know anything about it?'

'No, but I'll soon learn,' she assured him.

'Then what's more sensible than to have a manager while you do learn? Jared Wells knows a great deal about farming. He's travelled widely and has picked up knowledge all over the world.'

'I wouldn't say it was knowledge he's picked up. If he's so clever why isn't he running his own farm?'

Mr. Johnson leaned back and put his fingers together so that the tips touched.

'One has to admit,' he said, 'that Jared was improvident as a young man. He had good looks, wealthy, indulgent parents who made him think he could have anything he wanted and, one has heard, an attraction for women which also got him into trouble.'

Emma had difficulty controlling her indignation, for her temper was at flash point, but she could not vent it on this mild owl-like little man.

'I can't understand,' she said, trying to modulate her tone, 'how you can recommend to me that I have as manager a man who ran through his own money and, as you say, had a bad reputation with women.'

'No, no, you've misinterpreted me, Miss Page. Women ran after him. You can hardly blame him for that.'

'Can't I?' said Emma, seething. 'But anyhow, Mr. Johnson, tell me more about this condition. You say my uncle stipulated that Jared should remain as manager for two years. Have I got this right? Does he definitely say Jared, or would any manager do?'

'No, he particularly wanted Jared to remain as manager. He was always very fond of him, you know, and I think he believed that he had influenced Jared to take an interest in farming and lead a different kind of life. The Australians have leased the farm, Heron's Creek, for two years, so it all fits in well.'

'But not for me,' declared Emma, her lips mutinous. 'I can't think why on earth my Uncle Mac left the farm to me if I was going to be burdened with Jared's company day in and day out!'

'My dear young lady,' protested the attorney, 'he's a sound man now. I can see you remember him from your visit five years ago, but you didn't really know him, did you? There was a lot of gossip about him as there always is in a small community like this when someone has a personality that is, shall we say, a little different from the rest. I expect you had a bad impression of him from that, but, whatever was wrong then, he has put that all behind him, I can assure you.'

'I wonder. Leopards don't change their spots, you know, Mr. Johnson.'

'Why not give it a try, Miss Page? I'm sure you will find it very helpful to have a manager at first.'

'I agree – I might do,' said Emma. 'But not Jared Wells.

Is there no way I can get over this condition, Mr. Johnson?'

'Let me see. I didn't study it minutely because I hardly thought you would come here so quickly, if at all. Ah, yes, if within the said two years either of you should decide to marry and if your husband is interested in farming, you can break the terms of the will, or in the event Jared's proving unsuitable as a manager, you can with my permission dispense with his services.'

'Ah,' said Emma significantly.

'But, believe me, miss,' he went on, 'I consider Jared a very efficient manager. If you study the books for the last couple of years, you'll see I'm right.'

'But if he proved unsuitable in his behaviour?'

'I must say, Miss Page, that you seem to have a very distorted view of the man. I assure you that I would not advise you to retain him if I didn't consider him morally upright and of a great degree of integrity.'

Much he knows, thought Emma. He's just an old fuddy-duddy taken in by Jared's charm like everyone else.

'But if he did prove unsuitable?' she persisted.

'Well then, I must admit that I would have to advise you to dismiss him, but I hope this does not happen because running the farm has made a very great difference to Jared's way of life, and I think your uncle's idea was that he must keep on until he could take over his own farm again and make a success of it.'

'Has it occurred to you,' asked Emma, 'Mr. Johnson, that by the terms of this will, I have to live in the same house as Jared?'

'When your uncle made this will, Miss Page, I think he expected that your mother would accompany you. This was prior to her remarriage. But he's old enough to be your father, surely? It is not as if you'll be sharing the house with a young man.'

'But he's not my father!' declared Emma furiously.

'Dear me!' Mr. Johnson's blue eyes blinked owl-like through his spectacles. 'I understand that these days young ladies from London were not concerned with strict conventions and were proud of being able to look after themselves.'

'Of course I can look after myself, but I don't particularly want to live alone with this man sharing my house.'

'Then I would suggest that you advertise for a companion housekeeper.'

'I don't want a housekeeper – Rosie would give notice on the spot if I did that. And I don't need a companion. I couldn't be bothered with another woman around the place while I'm trying to learn about farming. No, Mr. Johnson, I'd looked forward to doing this on my own. I must say I'm bitterly disappointed at the way things have turned out.'

'Come, come, Miss Page, it's not as bad as that. If Jared had not taken over when he did you would have come here to find the farm in a very run-down condition. You should be grateful to him for all his work. I'm sure you will appreciate having him there when you know more about it and get to know him better. And as for the living arrangements, if you don't like having him in the house, surely there are suitable outhouses that could be made serviceable for him to live in. What about the place your uncle used to have as a museum? I think he used to sleep there sometimes. I remember seeing a camp bed.'

This is where I came in, thought Emma. Who would have thought that an old fellow like this would make me feel I'm being too conventional? It's obvious I won't get much help from him. I guess I'm the outsider here, and Jared is the favourite.

'Very well, Mr. Johnson,' she said. 'Let it rest for the time being. And now, if you would be good enough to explain the other details of the estate . . .'

When she came out of the office, she felt she knew a

good deal more about her affairs. It seemed true that a couple of years ago the farm had been going down and that gradually Jared had retrieved the position. It was by no means a wealthy place and there would be nothing to spare for quite a while, but it was gradually beginning to show more profit. No wonder Mr. Johnson had tried to dissuade her from getting rid of Jared! This, she felt, left her in a quandary. She did not want Jared, and yet it seemed as if she could not do without him.

Anyhow, there was one good thing that had emerged from her meeting with Mr. Johnson. She had asked him if she could buy a small secondhand car and he had given his consent. So before they returned to the farm, she was determined to have a look around the garages. A car would make her much more independent of Jared.

He was nowhere to be seen when she arrived back at the hotel in the town centre where they had arranged to have lunch. She went into the powder room and deciding she need not look so sedate any longer, took the pins from her hair and brushed it on to her shoulders.

'What a gorgeous shade your hair is! What colour shampoo do you use?' asked a voice behind her.

'I was born with this colour,' said Emma a little indignantly, turning to look at the girl who had taken a place beside her at the long mirror with its array of velvet and gilt stools.

'Dinkum?' asked the girl.

She was very blonde and Emma was tempted to ask her the same question, for it looked too good to be true, a kind of silver-gilt shade contrasted sharply with her even tan. She was wearing a pale apricot slacks suit, very well cut, and her dark brown eyes were like pansies, a complete and startling contrast to the colour of her hair.

'Are you Australian?' asked Emma.

'Too right I am. But we're living here for a few years. I wouldn't mind settling here for good. My pa's hired a

53

farm from one gorgeous hunk of a man. The only trouble is that we don't see enough of him lately. Someone's died and he's running this little farm for a while. But I'm hoping that won't last too long. I wish Pa could get him to manage for us, but my pop has got a bee in his bonnet about a back-to-the-land-stunt – wants to do it all himself. There's no need, because he's loaded. Isn't that crazy?'

'I don't think it is,' said Emma. 'I have ideas about running a farm on my own if anyone will let me.'

'Dinkum?' asked the girl, putting a cigarette between her scarlet newly made up lips. 'Heavens, you must be a devil for work! Me, I didn't take to the idea of being a farmer's girl back home because there's too damn much hard labour attached to it. But here it's a different story, of course. A farmer's wife is often better off than a townee, lots of servants, one nurse girl per child. Yes, I think I'll catch myself one of those gorgeous hunks of manhood you see around here and sit on my stoep and eat koeksusters and cream scones all day and grow the size of a house.'

'I have no ideas of being a farmer's wife,' said Emma. 'It's a farmer I want to be.'

'You must be joking,' said the girl. 'Oh, well, good-bye for now. Be seeing you.'

And that, thought Emma, must be the daughter of the Australian who has Jared's farm. She obviously fancies him. I must think about this. Maybe it's a way out of my troubles. She made her way back to the palm court where people were sitting having drinks before lunch. Still no sign of Jared. She wondered whether he was in the bar that in South Africa is reserved exclusively for the male sex. Well, she had no intention of sending a waiter to drag him out, if he was having a drink with the boys. She ordered a shandy and sat sipping it and watching the crowd who had come in for drinks and lunch. They all looked so clean, so sunburned and without a care in the world. No tension from fast living here, obviously.

A man detached himself from a group and approached her a little hesitantly.

'Isn't it Emma Page?' he asked. 'You may not remember me – I'm Terry Owen. I met you some years ago when you stayed at Sunglow.'

'Terry ... yes, of course, I remember you well,' smiled Emma.

He was what the Australian girl had described as a gorgeous hunk of a man, that is, he was about six foot tall, broad-shouldered, with large muscular arms and thighs of massive proportions. She had a vague idea that he had been a rugby player when she had known him before. He had grey eyes, brown close-cropped hair and the kind of lantern jaw and square back to the head that she associated with young South African men. With a great effort at recall she remembered that he had been one of her group of admirers, one of the more ardent ones, if a bit inarticulate.

'Do sit down,' she smiled. 'Lovely to see you.'

When Jared condescended to appear, he would find her fully occupied, she decided. Terry told the waiter to bring his beer over to her table and sat beaming at her.

'You're looking great,' he said. 'I heard old Mac had left the farm to you, but I thought it would be sold. We all expected old Jared would buy it. I expect you've come to see about it?'

Why had everyone in the district assumed she would sell the farm? She supposed Jared had had something to do with this idea.

'No, I've come back to live here,' she told him. 'I intend to run the farm.'

'Say, that's great. But what about Jared?'

'What about him?' asked Emma a bit sharply.

'Well, I mean to say, he's been running the farm for so long almost as if it were his own. In fact we all thought old Mac would leave it to him – I think he thought so too.

You could have knocked me down with a feather when I heard he'd left it to you.'

That would have taken some doing, thought Emma, regarding Terry's massive physique.

'If he'd had a male relative to leave it to, of course, that would have been understandable,' Terry went on, 'but to leave it to a girl . . . however, it's to be hoped you're going to get some help from Jared.'

'Yes, I expect I shall, like it or not,' said Emma. What a country! she thought. No one seems to know that women are emancipated. The idea of a woman running a farm seems to give everyone heart failure.

'I'm surprised he's willing to keep on at Sunglow, because he's very friendly with the people who are leasing his farm. Everyone thinks he'll marry the daughter, and then that would solve his problems. But old Jared's a wily bird. You never know where you are with him. Here he comes now. Look, how about coming to dinner and a show with me next week some time? I'll give you a ring.'

'I'd love to,' said Emma.

She would have hesitated if she had not been aware of the fact that Jared was near enough to hear the invitation and she had a childish desire to show him she was in demand.

'What would you love to do?' asked Jared, when the young man had gone back to his friends.

'Go to a dinner and show with Terry Owen next week. Any objections?' asked Emma pertly.

'Not particularly,' said Jared coolly. 'But if you really intend to put in a full day's work learning about farming, you won't have much time for play.'

'I'll make it for the week-end,' Emma promised.

Who's the owner, I would like to know? she thought. He speaks to me as if I'm an employee!

He ordered a beer, then sat back and looked at her. She was aware of his long fingers on the table near enough to touch, and those eyes, enigmatic, mysterious, dark. You never know where you are with him, Terry had said. How true that was!

'Well?' asked Jared.

Emma glanced up, her dark blue eyes meeting his with a wide-eyed innocent expression.

'Well what?' she said.

'You know very well what I mean,' he said. 'What did you think of the conditions of your uncle's will?'

'I was somewhat surprised,' she admitted silkily. 'But Mr. Johnson did his best to persuade me that everything is for the best.'

'I'm glad you think so,' said Jared.

He sounded a little puzzled. Perhaps he had expected more fight from her. But she had decided to appear reasonable until she had thought out a plan of campaign. She was still determined to get rid of this man, and the sooner the better.

'We're joining some friends of mine for lunch, the ones who are hiring Heron's Creek,' Jared told her.

He could have asked me if I minded, Emma thought. She was childishly disappointed that she was not to have lunch alone with him and that was stupid, considering her previous thoughts. But when she was here before it had been considered a great treat to have lunch in town at this hotel, and there had been something alluring about the idea of having her first meal here dressed in her best and with a very handsome man.

As they went into the crowded dining room, many heads turned to inspect Emma and Jared and there was a ripple of conversation. Emma remembered that any new arrival received the same treatment in this little town. The major domo directed them to a table in the circular bay window overlooking the garden of the town centre.

'Jared, you're here at last! I thought you were never coming.'

The silver blonde girl sprang up to greet him. She had obviously been waiting for him eagerly. Her father, a ruddy grey-haired man, rose slightly as Emma was introduced.

'This is Yolande Mitchell and her father, Craig, Emma,' said Jared.

'But we've met before. It was you in the powder room, wasn't it?' exclaimed Yolande. 'Oh, goodness, are you the owner of Sunglow?' She turned around accusingly. 'Jared, you never told me she was so glam. You gave me the idea she was some insignificant Limey who wouldn't even be interested in coming here.'

'I don't know what gave you that impression, Yolande, my dear,' Jared answered, smoothly passing over the awkward moment. 'I admit I didn't think she would come, and I'd forgotten how attractive Emma was. She was only sixteen when I last saw her and she'd hardly grown up then.'

Does he really remember so little about it? Emma marvelled. She did not like to be talked about as if she were not there.

'But are you really going to stay and run Sunglow?' asked Yolande, her thin pencilled brows raised above the pansy brown eyes.

'That's my intention,' said Emma firmly.

'You're fortunate to have Jared to help you.'

'So everyone tells me,' said Emma drily.

'He's put a terrific amount of work into the farm, hasn't he, Pa?' Yolande went on. 'I call it a crying shame that he didn't get it left to him.'

'Now, Yolly love, don't say things that might give offence. It's nothing to do with us, after all,' said Mr. Mitchell placatingly. 'Let's all sit down and order our lunch. Where's that wine waiter?'

During the meal Yolande did her best to monopolize Jared, and Emma talked to Craig Mitchell, who seemed a pleasant enough man, but quite obsessed with his lovely daughter. Emma had to listen to long stories of her beauty and talents that she had possessed, according to her doting father, since she was a tiny child. However, when lunch was over, Jared was called away on some business about an implement he had ordered, and when Mr. Mitchell had gone away too, Yolande began to concentrate her attention upon Emma.

'Did you bring someone with you?' she asked. 'I believe your mother was with you last time?'

'No, she has remarried. I'm here alone,' Emma told her.

'Alone? But haven't you got a fiancé you intend to marry? You don't intend to live there by yourself, do you?'

Emma felt mischievous under this cross-examination.

'No boy-friend, unfortunately. But of course I'm not alone at Sunglow. There's Jared.'

The colour on Yolande's face, already vivid, darkened to an angry red.

'He isn't sleeping there?' she demanded.

'Where else?' asked Emma. 'There's no manager's house.'

'Well,' said Yolande, 'I don't think that's very good for your reputation, Miss...'

'Call me Emma.'

'Emma, you can't know what a small town is like for gossip. I feel quite concerned for you. I can't help feeling you shouldn't have Jared sleeping in the same house.'

Emma, who had been making this point so emphatically to Mr. Johnson just a little while before, was amused to find herself taking the opposite view just to annoy this young lady who seemed so possessive with Jared.

'No one need know,' she smiled sweetly. 'It can be our little secret, Yolande. Do you mind if I call you that?'

'I'm only telling you this for your own good,' Yolande said crossly. 'You don't know the place. Anything creates a scandal, specially if it has to do with Jared. He's charming, you know, Emma, but I don't know that one can trust him where women are concerned.'

'How exciting you make him sound!' purred Emma.

Yolande glared at her.

'I've heard that they're very permissive in London, but this isn't London here, you know. It might spoil your chances of marriage if people know you're living with Jared.'

'Oh, dear, do you really think so?' asked Emma, pretending to look worried.

'Yes, I do. I tell you what I'll do,' said Yolande. 'I can see it's very difficult for you in the circumstances. I'll ask Pa if he'd mind if Jared came to live at Heron's Creek. It's not far from Sunglow and he could drive over every day. I'm sure Pa will say yes. He'll do anything for me.'

'I think you'd better ask Jared first,' said Emma.

CHAPTER FOUR

'WHAT gave you the idea that I would be willing to stay at Heron's Creek?' asked Jared when they were alone again.

'It wasn't exactly my idea,' Emma protested.

'You must have had a real girls together talk with Yolande for her to offer me a bed there,' he insisted. 'Why the hell couldn't you have kept quiet about the fact that we're sharing the house? Next thing everyone will be saying we're sleeping together.'

'For heaven's sake,' exclaimed Emma, 'who was it who moaned about the camp bed in the museum?'

'Well, if you're going to be so prissy and complain to everyone you meet that I've got dishonourable intentions, I'll get the museum cleaned out and a bed moved over there,' snapped Jared.

'Please do,' said Emma. 'That will suit me fine.'

She felt furious that somehow she had been given the blame for Yolande's suggestion, when she knew perfectly well that all the Australian girl wanted was to see more of Jared and to get him for herself.

'I've finished all the business in town,' said Jared. 'We can go home now.'

'But I haven't finished,' Emma protested. 'I'm going to look at the garages.'

'Whatever for?' he asked.

'I intend to buy a car. You may come with me if you wish.'

'Who said you could buy a car?'

'I wasn't aware that I needed anyone's permission, but as a matter of fact I did ask Mr. Johnson if the estate could run to it.'

'And I suppose the old fool said "Certainly, Miss Page,

go and buy yourself a Rolls Royce!" Old men can never resist a pretty face.'

'There's no need to be sarcastic!' she snapped. 'I need a small car that will take me for short distances. I can't be stuck on the farm the whole time. I need to be independent.'

'So this is the way it's going to go, is it?' drawled Jared.

'What do you mean?'

'You're going to spend money on things that are not necessary for the farm. I thought you were so keen to keep it going.'

'Of course I am, but, Jared, please credit me with a bit of sense. Mr. Johnson has explained the financial position to me and I think it will run to a secondhand Mini. If not I'll have to substitute for one of the packers when the time comes and save the wages.'

'You couldn't do that. You don't know enough about it.'

'But I shall by that time,' Emma assured him. 'I intend to know all about the farm, and the sooner the better. Now, are you going to take me around the garages, Jared, or must I walk?'

'God preserve me from a redhead mistress!' Jared exclaimed. 'Come along, then. If you're so determined to spend your money, I'd better come with you to see that you don't get swindled.'

They found a small mini station wagon that was for sale because the owner had bought a bigger model. It was useful to have Jared around, Emma had to admit, for the garage men obviously respected him and he was able to get a firm promise that they would fix various defects before she took delivery.

'I had thought I would be able to drive it back,' she said as they set off again to go back to the farm.

'Impatient, aren't you? Or do you just want to be rid of my company?'

'Whatever gave you that idea?' asked Emma.

Out of the town the tarred road petered out and Jared had to concentrate on avoiding the potholes and corrugations. She could look at him now without being afraid he would intercept her gaze. Do I want to get rid of his company? she asked herself. Yes, definitely. I'd be much better without him. I can't stand that, in spite of the fact that he's quite infuriating and has such a very high opinion of himself and opposes me in every way, he still exercises this charm on me as he does, it seems, to every woman in the district under seventy. He has this almost hypocritical type of charisma that has nothing to do with whether you dislike or like him. Look at him now, those black brows frowning a little, his features so complete and satisfying, his brown hands on the wheel, relaxed and confident, his arms, those arms that once held me so close to him, strong, brown, with their light sprinkling of black hairs. I must stop thinking about it, she thought, but how can I help it?

'Why didn't you accept Yolande's invitation to sleep there?' she asked.

'I prefer to be on the spot. I promised old Mac I would look after the farm and, by God, I shall, even if it includes an obstinate redhead.'

She did not give him the satisfaction of a reply. Instead she began to think over her conversation with Mr. Johnson. The condition that Jared should stay as manager fell away if either of them married. She considered her own future. A husband did not figure in her scheme of things. When she had heard that she had inherited the farm, she had been delighted and indulged in many daydreams about her life there, but no one else had had any part in them. It would be so lovely, she had thought, to leave the rather monotonous office job she had been doing and to get away on her own. She had made all sorts of plans about what she would do, for she

63

was never bored with her own company. She knew it would be hard work on the farm, but there must be some times when she would have leisure and she had thought that, in addition to riding and playing tennis, she would be able to do other things, maybe convert the old museum into a studio where she would try her hand at painting, perhaps have a kiln and learn to do pottery.

Could she try to attract one of the local farmers? It seemed a heavy price to pay to marry in haste just to get rid of one's manager. There must be some easier way. Men had told her she was attractive since she was sixteen, but the only man who had thrilled her at all was the man at her side. Goodness knows why, for he had all the qualities she most disliked. He was arrogant, overbearing and a philanderer as well. Five years ago, she thought, I was too young to resist him, but now I know better. It's early days yet. Perhaps I shall meet some farmer who's charming and wealthy and suitable. What pleasure it would give me to tell Jared I don't require his services any longer. But what about Jared? Can't I get him married off to someone?

'Do you find Yolande attractive?' she asked before she could stop herself.

He smiled lazily and glanced across at her.

'Why are you sitting bolt upright and so far away from me? I won't bite. Yolande . . . ah, yes . . . now she wouldn't sit like that. Yes, certainly, Yolande has what it takes, a passable face, a lovely figure, and a rich father, and – wait for it – an extra bonus.'

'What bonus?' asked Emma. She was surprised to find herself becoming cross, for it was she who had started the conversation.

'An amorous disposition,' said Jared, still smiling.

'Don't smirk like that,' snapped Emma furiously. 'How do you know?'

'I just do. Men know these things.'

'Have you . . . have you kissed her?'

'My dear Emma, you sound sixteen again! And if I have, is there any rule in our contract or any condition in the will to say I may not make love to any woman I please?'

'You can make love to the whole district for all I care. Just so long as you count me out.

'What an iceberg you turned out to be, Emma!' he grinned. 'Astonishing. Delving in my memories, I wouldn't have said you would be such a little acid-drop.'

'I can't be both. I doubt whether you remember anything about me.'

'You'd be surprised. Some girls make more impression than others.'

He drew the car to a halt under a giant wild fig tree at the side of the road.

'Why are you stopping?' asked Emma.

'I can't keep my mind on the road if you are determined to argue with me.'

'Who's arguing? Does Yolande make more impression than others?'

'I was speaking about you, not Yolande. Yes, I remember you well, Emma, fresh, beautiful, unspoiled – and devastatingly innocent. You made me feel like some old roué, decadent, and dissipated.'

'And were you?' asked Emma.

He had turned to face her, but she could not read the expression in those dark eyes. He put out his hand and touched her cheek.

'No, Emma, perhaps a bit too eager to live, to experience all things, perhaps a spot wild. But what man worth anything has not been wild in his youth?'

'Your youth has lasted a long time, Jared.'

His hand dropped from her cheek.

'But Emma's sweetness didn't, it's evident. What's happened to you, Emma? What's made you so hard? Or is

65

this how women are in England these days?'

'You make me tired when you talk in that way!' she snapped. 'It's perfectly true what someone on the plane said, "We are now arriving in South Africa. Turn back your watch twenty-five years." Only in your case I think it's more like a hundred. I never met with more anti-quated ideas! Just because I'm not prepared to say, "Yes, Jared, no, Jared, just as you say because you know best, Jared," you say I'm hard and modern and goodness knows what else. I'm not at all hard, but I'm perfectly capable of looking after myself, as every modern girl should be.'

Jared put his hands on her shoulders and then suddenly they had slid around her and she was in his embrace. His mouth was smiling.

'Are you, Emma. Are you sure?'

His long fingers sought her cheek and slid down from there to the soft curve of her neck and the delicate hollow at the base of her throat, then gently, almost imper-ceptibly, rested on the curve of her left breast. Her mouth came up to the firm line of his that was hard and sure upon her own yielding one. Her swimming senses were quivering in response to his demanding passion – and yet somewhere in the distance small urgent alarm signals were sending out a warning that she did not want to hear.

When the long kiss was over, her mouth sought his again and she clung to him, softly tracing the outline of his lips with her own. The warning notes flashed brightly in her brain and she tore herself away from him and sought the far corner of the seat.

'I thought I told you,' she said shakily, 'that I didn't appreciate casual lovemaking.'

He was smiling, and this suddenly enraged her. Oh, how could she betray herself by responding to him in the way she had? She thought he must put her in the same class as Yolande and all the other girl-friends who yielded to his charm so easily.

'It seemed to me,' he said, 'that you weren't actually hating it. And I'm so glad to know that the young Emma I remember hasn't vanished for ever.'

'This Emma is certainly not prepared to add herself to your list of conquests,' Emma replied sharply. She smoothed her hair and sat up as straight as possible. 'Please let's drive on, Jared. I would like to see something of the farm before sunset.'

'Yes, madam, anything you say,' said Jared.

He drove away with a slight smile on those lips that she had clung to only a few minutes before. He's got to go, she told herself. That's absolutely certain. She was glad when at last she saw the welcoming sight of Sunglow, resting peacefully amongst its blossoming trees.

'I'll take these supplies in to the kitchen and tell Rosie we need tea,' said Jared, when they arrived. 'You'd better change out of that expensive-looking outfit if you want to see some of the farm.'

I don't need his advice, she thought rebelliously, but she went up to her room and changed into denim jeans and a matching jacket. This outfit, instead of making her look tough, somehow emphasized her femininity, the round curves of her hips and the fragility of her small fine-boned face above the shirtlike top.

Rosie had brought the tea out on to the stoep and they sat on the wrought iron chairs where the grapevine dappled the shade of its young leaves upon the uneven stones. Emma was glad that they were not sitting in the more intimate atmosphere of the living-room with its deep settee. She sat up primly on the hard seat, pouring tea and trying not to look at Jared, but all the time she was aware that he was watching her intently.

Finally he said, 'What's the matter, Emma? Why are you so quiet? Are you going to pretend that that kiss never happened?'

'I would prefer to,' Emma admitted. 'Jared, I don't

67

find it amusing that you should play games with me. As long as we have to live here like this, I want you to remember. . . .'

'My place,' Jared suggested. 'All right, Emma, whatever you say.'

She looked up, surprised by his meek reply, and caught the dark smouldering glance that denied what he was saying.

'It seems I can't get rid of you yet,' she said. 'So I'd be pleased if you would. . . .'

'Conduct myself with circumspection,' Jared suggested. 'All right, Emma dear, I promise you I'll not do anything that you don't want me to.'

She glanced at him suspiciously. Was there a gleam of laughter in those dark eyes? She knew she had betrayed herself by her response to his kiss. And now how could she make this right?

'I'm not a nun, Jared,' she said sedately.

'I'm glad of that, Emma,' he replied without a smile.

'I mean that sometimes a girl appears to respond because she hasn't been kissed for a while and really it doesn't mean a thing.'

'I'm always glad to have information on women,' said Jared. 'I must confess they're puzzling at times.'

'I thought you thought you knew all about them,' Emma accused him.

'Quite a lot, but not all.'

Jared was smiling now. She supposed he had been laughing at her all the time. She got to her feet.

'Please show me around the farm,' she commanded him.

And yet when they had set out she realized that it was not a particularly good time to view the farm because the farmhands were packing up for the night and soon she and Jared were alone beneath the dazzling western sky. It would have been better if she had waited until the morning. Now she was too conscious of the man at her side as they walked towards the orchards. A lone ibis flapped overhead shouting with his raucous note as if to say to the rest of the flock, 'Wait for me!' and egrets descended on to the poplar trees and rested there like huge white flowers.

'Why do we grow so many poplars?' Emma asked. 'I thought they weren't so good for the ground?'

'They're all right if you watch the roots,' he explained. 'We have to have suitable trees for a windbreak to protect the fruit. When they get too large we can sell them to a match factory.'

Emma was glad that they were having a practical conversation, for now as she approached the orchards, the fragrance of the blossom came towards them in wafts that were heartbreakingly sweet. They reminded her of the time when she had been here before and she felt a sad nostalgia for the years that had passed. Oh, what had happened to the eager ardent child who had wanted to experience everything? The chill of disillusion at that early age had been like a touch of frost upon the blossoming gold of youth.

Blossoming gold? Yes, it was all around her now. They had entered a pathway between the trees that were laden with white fragrant flowers on either side. The sun was going down and sending shafts of golden light between the branches so that each petal was touched with radiance. Here and there oranges left from the previous crop shone like lamps amidst the blossom and against the background of shiny dark green leaves.

'I'd forgotten how lovely it is when the trees are in blossom,' said Emma, gently touching a branch, then pulling it towards her to breathe in the heavenly scent. Now she thought, he'll probably say something about spraying for pests or irrigation, or at any rate something practical to spoil my perfect moment. But he did not. He stood looking at her, a dark, clearcut silhouette against the golden blaze of the western sky. His black hair was touched with light and his skin was golden like a sun god's. He looked remote and mysterious not at all the teasing man she had argued with all day. She was suddenly aware of the loneliness around them, the vast sweeps of uninhabited country, the darkening sky with one bright star and a crescent moon becoming more clearly defined as the sunset gave way reluctantly to the fast descending night.

He took a step forward and grasped both her hands in his. 'Lovely golden Emma,' he said. 'You can't know how utterly beautiful you look with the light on your hair and that background of blossom.'

She was in his arms without knowing how she got there and they were kissing as they had kissed five long years ago. His hands slid underneath the rough material of the denim jacket and her back felt shudderingly smooth beneath his caresses. She felt him lift her gently and then she was lying on the turf beneath the dark shade of the orange trees. The fragrant scent of the crushed grass seemed to bring some bittersweet nostalgia, but she did not heed it. She was only astonished at her own desire, her lack of shame as those slender hands caressed her with experienced skill. Her eyes were closed, for she knew she could not bear to meet that dark ardent gaze.

'Look at me, Emma,' he commanded. 'I made a promise to you that I would do nothing against your will. Is this what you want?'

She nodded her head, for she could not bring herself to speak. Far in the distance there was the sound of a bell. It broke through the waves of emotion that had threatened to engulf her in their deep waters. She opened her eyes and dared to look at him. His eyes seemed to glow like a panther's in the dark and she was suddenly terribly afraid.

'It's impossible, Jared. We're quite crazy to be like this!'

His ardent lips sought hers once more, but she turned her head away.

'I don't feel crazy,' he said. 'I'm being very sensible, I thought.'

She got to her feet and grasped at a tree because she found she was trembling too much to stand.

'Sensible?' she asked, as he rose and came to her side. 'I suppose you think it's sensible to make the most of being alone with any woman. But, Jared, two can play at this game. I got an assurance from Mr. Johnson that if he finds you're not suitable to stay here, if your behaviour is bad, I can get the terms of the will altered.'

She was speaking wildly, scarcely knowing what she was saying, grasping at any exuse that would explain her surrender to her senses and to his ardent lovemaking, but he had put his arm around her to steady her and she felt the muscles go rigid.

'I could have sworn . . .!' he said. 'No matter, Emma. Now I know where I stand with you. There's Rosie's bell ringing again. Let's go back to the house.'

Emma found it difficult to break the silence as they walked back and with a murmured excuse she went quickly to her room. She looked at her reflection and saw a woman dishevelled with brilliant colour and huge dark blue eyes. She looked almost as if she had a fever. What had possessed her to trust herself to go with Jared at that time and to behave in the way she had? She shuddered at the thought that so nearly he had added her to his list of conquests.

What could she do? She knew that to show her attraction to Jared would be fatal, and yet when she thought of his lovemaking, and of how she had felt when those sensitive long fingers caressed her skin, she trembled and longed for his hands. How could she face him across the dinner table? And yet she must. She would have to go on, and try to pretend that she had deliberately led him on so that she could plead that his behaviour was unsuitable for that of a manager to her farm. So she must brazen it out.

71

She could not let him see that his passionate advances had shaken her so much that she had forgotten she had meant to maintain a frigid poise in her dealings with him.

And yet the other side of her longed for his approval, still wanted to appear attractive to him, and she changed from her denim jeans and put on a long cotton skirt with a dark background and small sprays of gay flowers together with a simple pale blue blouse with a casual shirt neckline open at the front. He had changed too, she noticed, when she came down, although she had not heard him in his room. Perhaps she had been too absorbed in her own thoughts. He was wearing slim-fitting camel-coloured slacks and a casual cream shirt that emphasised his dark colouring. Emma's heart jerked unbearably when she saw how handsome he appeared. Why should his physical self have so much effect on her? And yet it did. He appeared suave, completely unruffled by their scene in the orchard, and he offered her sherry again, acting as if he were her host and she were his guest.

'A sherry will calm your nerves, my dear Emma. Sit here and calm down. You look agitated.'

'I'm not in the least agitated,' she retorted. 'Please, Jared, let's forget this afternoon as quickly as possible if we're to continue to stay together.'

'Just as you please,' he replied coldly.

I suppose he's not used to being refused, Emma thought. Oh, why did I let myself in for all this confusing emotion? She sat as far away from him as possible and sipped at her sherry. She was conscious of his dark eyes upon her but would not look at him.

'Come, Emma,' he said finally. 'You're no longer a little girl. Why behave so primly about something that was rather lovely? Even if you did intend to lead me on in the first place with the idea of making me behave badly, you can't deny that there was some feeling on your part, isn't that so? Admit that you like me a little, otherwise this would never have happened.'

Emma shook her head. The sensible side of her felt she must not be led astray by his facile excuses, that were just intended, she was sure, to make it easier for him to go on making love to her, whenever he felt like it.

'That isn't true. I don't like you at all, Jared. I insist that as long as you have to stay here this must be a completely business relationship. You're just seizing the opportunity to try to attract me because I'm here on the spot and easily available, but, strange as it may seem to you, I don't indulge in promiscuous behaviour. I don't want any more to do with you.'

He was about to reply when they heard the sound of a car in the driveway, a door slammed shut and they heard someone coming through the hall without using the lion's head that served as a knocker. Yolande sauntered into the room, her hips swaying with that subtle sexy walk that Emma had noticed when they met at lunch.

'Hi, Jared, hi, Emma. I suddenly had a bright idea on my way home that I could call in here and collect Jared for dinner. There are several things Pop wants to discuss about the farm. You haven't eaten yet, have you? I've hired a home movie from town and we can watch that afterwards, Jared. It's a real hot number. You'll love it.'

Jared looked at Emma. His expression had been dark with fury at her last remark, but now he smiled at the other girl.

'That sounds great, Yolande, it'll suit me fine. I won't be a second. I must collect a jacket. Shall I bring my car?'

'No, of course not, Jared darling. I'll love to drive you home, you know that.'

Jared went upstairs and Yolande sat on the arm of a chair and looked Emma up and down.

'You're looking glam, Emma. What a dinky skirt! Are you expecting anyone, or was this all for Jared's benefit?' She did not wait for a reply but went on, 'You don't mind if I take Jared away for the evening, do you?'

'Not in the least,' said Emma. She felt like adding, You can take him for ever for all I care.

'It wouldn't be much fun for you if I included you too, would it? Two's company and all that jazz.'

'Jared is my manager, not my husband,' said Emma stiffly. 'He's perfectly free to do as he pleases.'

'That's great, then. I didn't think you would mind. I'm crazy about Jared, I don't mind telling you, and Pop thinks he's God's gift to Africa. Maybe one of these days I shall get him on the hook.'

'I wish you luck,' Emma said smoothly.

She watched them drive away in the girl's smart sports car and then went into the kitchen to tell Rosie to serve dinner. The old servant had set the table in the dining-room and Emma sat alone surrounded by the stiff expressions of her ancestors. Rosie shook her head because so much of her well cooked dinner was left over, but Emma found it difficult to eat. She selected a book from the shelves at the side of the fireplace and went to bed early, but, sitting up in bed in the virginal room with the yellow roses, she found she did not know what she was reading.

She wished desperately that Jared had not come back into her life. Perhaps Yolande was a solution to her problem – and yet when she thought of the two of them together in the night she felt a piercing flash of pain. How could she be so foolish? At last she slept, and if Jared came into the next room that night she did not even hear him. But perhaps he had stayed with Yolande. She longed desperately to know if he had.

CHAPTER FIVE

AFTER her restless night, Emma slept late and woke to the sound of some commotion in the passage outside her room. Putting on her dressing-gown, she opened the door and saw Rosie supervising the removal of the bed from Jared's room.

'What are you doing, Rosie?' she asked, though it was rather obvious what was happening.

'Baas Jared he say you don't like him sleep here, Miss Emma. He say he must move to museum. But, Miss Emma, why not like? Baas Jared good man, nice and strong. If skellum come here, he could fight him. Many bad people around in this country. Not good to stay alone.'

'I prefer to be by myself in the house, Rosie,' Emma replied rather coldly.

'Ai, Miss Emma, woman needs man. Not good to stay be self. Perhaps if you speak nice to Baas Jared he might marry you.'

'I don't think so, Rosie. Now, I must go and bath. I just want toast and orange juice for breakfast. I'll be down soon.'

'All right, Miss Emma, but if you don't marry him, that Miss Yolande will.'

Feeling ruffled, Emma went to bath and dress. She put on the denim outfit she had discarded last night. She was determined to get a good look at the farm this morning. I've had enough of emotion, she thought. Today everything must be very practical. I came here to run this farm and I'm going to do it!

But when she got down there was Jared at the breakfast table helping himself to a large plate of lamb chops, bacon and eggs from the sideboard. In spite of her good resolutions, her heart leapt when she saw him. He spoke as if he had no recollection of their scene last night.

'Good morning, Emma. Rosie said you only wanted toast, but I told her to bring a proper breakfast for you as I intend to show you around the farm this morning and you'll need your strength. I can't have a fainting farmer on my hands, can I?'

How dared he grin so wickedly? She had a good mind to say she would not come. And yet what could she do? There was no one else who could explain things to her. To her surprise she was able to eat the bacon and eggs he insisted on putting on to her plate.

'Did you enjoy your visit to Heron's Creek?' she asked.

'Moderately,' Jared answered. 'Craig Mitchell is worried about the dam that irrigates both our farms.'

Emma was surprised that the conversation had taken such a practical turn. She longed to know more about his feelings for Yolande, but evidently he was being discreet.

'Where is the dam?' she asked.

'Through the forests and in a hollow of the mountains a few miles away. We think we'll have to get an engineer to see about it. It seems to have developed a couple of cracks and that might not be so good with the rainy season approaching.'

'Will it be costly to have it mended?'

'Naturally. Anything of that kind must be costly these days. However, it's no good crossing our bridges. In any case you needn't worry, because I think old Mac made some provision in case something of this kind happened.'

'Did you . . . did Yolande bring you home?'

'Yes, Emma, she did.'

Jared smiled as if recalling something pleasant, and Emma had a furious urge to hit that smile from his face.

'She seems to like you,' she said, trying to sound sweet.

'Oh, yes, indeed. Most women do, Emma. You're the

exception that proves the rule.'

His dark eyes were alight with glittering laughter. How dared he goad her like this?

'I'd hate to be one of a crowd,' she told him.

'Beautiful, gorgeous Emma, lovely redhaired Emma, how could you ever be one of a crowd?' he asked. 'But I hope you realize how well I'm behaving now? I've removed myself to the museum and now I'm to sleep with all those horrific African souvenirs instead of next door to my lovely Emma. That should teach me not to follow my impulses, shouldn't it?'

'I don't want to talk about it any more,' Emma said shortly.

Now that he had taken things out of her hands, she was not sure that she had really wanted things this way. Certainly she had not imagined that he would remove himself so completely. But why did she feel let down and disappointed? Her whole aim since she had come here was to get rid of him from the farm. But this was different. He was still here and yet apart from her. She would still see him, and how was she to get over this stupid attraction she felt for him if she saw him every day?

The countryside looked quite different in the light of day. The sky was that deep azure blue that is so startling to someone brought up to the softer colours of a northern climate, and the mountains were hazy with the promise of heat to come. Below the young trees the soil was red and loamy. Jared had provided her with a chestnut horse and he was riding a black one with a white blaze that was very similar to the one he had had those five years ago.

'I keep my horses here,' he told her. 'Do you remember Satan? This is a younger edition, his son in fact.'

Emma had a flash of memory. Once again she was a young girl waiting beside the river, seeing this man riding like a matador towards her. Once again she felt the quivering thrill of that first morning. He had not changed, but she had. She had become a woman, mature and sensible, she hoped.

The young trees were being irrigated and Emma was introduced to several coloured workers who were supervising this. The water was led from the river by pump and mechanical sprays watered the saplings and the crops of vegetables that were growing in the rich alluvial soil by the river banks.

'We're fortunate to share this part of the river between us,' said Jared. 'Citrus thrives in this light sandy loam, and the alluvial soils contain an abundance of organic matter that's good for the trees.'

'What about drainage?' asked Emma, for she was determined to sound intelligent. Jared smiled.

'Luckily we have no problems that way. Waterlogged soil makes trees more liable to diseases of the root system.'

'What about pests and so on . . . do you have to spray a lot?' asked Emma.

'Constantly. During the fruiting season, the orchards have to be watched all the time and have to be sprayed and powdered to protect the fruit from insects, fungi and disease. Oh, yes, Emma, orange trees take a great deal of labour. You can never leave them alone.'

'But isn't the spray bad for the fruit?'

'It's all carefully washed off before they're exported.'

Down the aisles of blossoming trees the water was ascending in sparkling jets and the sun catching them in its light transformed them into a hundred rainbows.

'Each tree has to be given about two thousand to four thousand litres every three or four weeks in the spring and early summer. We can't rely on rainfall here,' Jared explained.

By the time they had ridden around a great part of the farm, Emma had begun to think that maybe after all Mr. Johnson had been correct in saying it would be useful to have a manager for a while. There was so much she had to learn. But of course the manager need not necessarily be Jared, from her point of view. And yet she could not imagine what it would be like to employ someone else. But she did not want to come to rely on him, for then she would never get rid of him. It seemed, however, that the whole thing might be taken out of her hands and that Yolande would marry him. She could not imagine that Yolande would tolerate for one day that he should remain as manager here once she had become engaged to him.

They had brought a few sandwiches and coffee with them and when they came to the river bank Jared called a halt to the farming demonstration and suggested they should sit in the shade of the trees. Did he remember that it was the exact spot where they had first spoken to each other five long years ago? Probably not. Men don't remember things like that, Emma thought, and anyhow he could hardly have any sentimental recollections about it. Nor have I, she assured herself firmly.

'No apples today?' said Jared, breaking into her thoughts. So he did remember!

'Did you want apples?' she asked innocently.

'Not particularly, but I recall a young lovely Emma offering one to me a long time ago. She looked like Eve and was just as tempting – except of course that she had more clothes on.'

'That's just the kind of remark I would expect from you. Don't you ever connect women with anything but sex?' asked Emma.

'Yes, food,' said Jared promptly. 'I like them to be able to cook well too.'

'Can Yolande cook?'

'Why do we always have to get on to the subject of Yolande? You seem obsessed with the girl, Emma.'

'I thought you were,' she retorted.

'Not I. I have yet to meet a woman who could obsess me. But meanwhile I guess Yolande will have to do.'

'I suppose she's more accommodating than me,' said Emma furiously.

'Yes, definitely. She would never banish me to a museum.'

It was infuriating that although she knew very well that Jared was trying to bait her, she should not be able to ignore his teasing and that he could make her feel so angry.

'I wish you'd make up your mind to marry her,' she said crossly.

'So you could get rid of me? Well, who knows, perhaps I shall. She's good fun and doesn't get as difficult as one person I could name. But of course, I forgot, you're my mistress, not my future wife.'

He was sitting beside her and as he turned to look at her she could feel the hard muscles of his thigh against the softness of her own. Before she knew what he was doing he had her face cupped in his slender brown hands.

'You look so lovely when you're angry with me,' he said. 'Your eyes are almost black, deep, deep cobalt, but sparkling with little diamonds. I almost expect that fiery hair to rise all around your head like a lion's mane. Sweet Emma, what makes you oppose me? You're missing so much joy.'

'I've told you already that I'm not willing to count myself as one of your conquests, Jared,' she snapped. 'Isn't it enough that I have to put up with you as manager without this constant siege on my person?'

Jared laughed. She felt his body shake, vibrant and vigorous beside her, or was it her own body trembling?

'You make yourself sound like Mafeking. Siege of your person, indeed! Let me tell you, Emma, that I've never yet made love to a woman against her will. One day you'll admit to me that you enjoy my kisses and ask for more.'

'Here's someone else who might oblige you,' Emma replied caustically as she saw a figure approaching through the trees.

'Cooee, you two! I came over to the house, but Rosie told me you were somewhere around the farm. You don't look very hardworking, I must say.'

Yolande was dressed in very abbreviated blue shorts and a top tied under her breasts leaving her brown waist bare. Her silver-blonde curls were gathered up into a topknot and a sunhat swung from her hand.

'I think Emma has had enough instruction for one day, Yolande,' said Jared. 'Too much could confuse her.'

'Is that what you call it?' Yolande pouted. 'Instruction in what? It looked quite interesting as I was coming along. No wonder you say it might confuse her, Jared. How about a little instruction for me too?'

Emma hated the idea that Yolande had seen them sitting together in that intimate pose.

'I'll go back to the house,' she said. 'You two can follow later. Can you stay for lunch, Yolande? I'll tell Rosie.'

'Just a bit of salad for me, thanks, Emma. I'm dieting.'

As Emma made her way back, she realized that she had forgotten that Jared had said he would eat alone. Perhaps he would be annoyed that he could not have Yolande to himself. Well, she would see that she left them on their own in future.

But they did not need any encouragement at this, she thought, as she heard laughter and talk coming from the open door of the museum building some time later. Evidently Jared must have told Yolande about his new sleeping arrangements. She wished he had not. When they finally came in and were sitting on the stoep having a pre-lunch beer, Yolande had the look of a Persian kitten who had found a saucer of cream. When Jared was called to the phone, she took the opportunity of saying to Emma, 'I think it's very wise, Emma, that

81

Jared has gone across to the museum to sleep. You never know who'll find out and gossip about you two being alone here.'

'Perhaps you'd like to take him off my hands, Yolande?' Emma remarked smoothly. 'When I've learned a bit more about the farm, I would appreciate being free of him.'

'Truly? You surprise me, Emma. Why, I should think all the woman in the district are drooling with envy of you because you have him on your doorstep. I am, for one.'

Jared returned from the hallway. He was smiling. Had he heard any of their conversation? Emma wondered.

'Your car is ready. I'll take you in to fetch it this afternoon,' he said.

'I can take her,' said Yolande quickly. 'I have a hairdressing appointment anyway. I'm sure you have lots that you want to do, Jared. You haven't time for running Emma around all the time.'

'That's exactly why I've bought a car,' said Emma. 'Thank you, Yolande, I'd love to come with you.'

'And I shall come too,' Jared declared. 'I must see that they've done all the things to the car that were necessary before we take delivery, and I'll pick up a spare part I need at the same time.'

Yolande looked annoyed.

'It takes ages to get my hair done, Jared. I know you won't have the patience to wait around.'

'I won't have to. Emma can drive me home. I'll entrust myself to her driving.'

'That's big of you,' said Emma.

As she drove her little car back to the farm, with herself at the wheel, she felt rather pleased with herself. While she was waiting for Jared to collect the spare part for the tractor, she had seen Terry Owen again and had made a date with him for dinner in town at the week-end. As he had been talking to her, Jared came out of the spares department and greeted Terry in a rather offhand manner.

'We can get going now, Emma. I want to get this spare fixed before dark,' he said abruptly. Terry took the hint and waved gaily as they started off.

'See you on Saturday, Emma,' he shouted.

'And what did he mean by that?' asked Jared.

'Don't talk to me for a moment while I sort out these gears. Terry ...? I'm going to have dinner with him on Saturday and go to a cinema. At least I think that's the idea.'

'Well, take my advice and don't go to the drive-in.'

'Why not?'

'Because it will give friend Terry ample opportunity for making love to you – and of course you wouldn't like that, would you?'

'How do you know I wouldn't?' she demanded.

'From bitter experience. But, Emma, a friendly warning. Don't lead him on. Not all men will take no for an answer.'

Emma crashed the gears.

'Now look what you've made me do! Really, Jared, give me credit for being able to look after myself, and as for leading him on —most men, I find – don't need much leading. They're usually there before me.'

They drove on in silence for some miles.

'For a woman driver, you're not at all bad, I must say, Emma,' said Jared, when she had had to change down on a steep hill to avoid a milling, confused and confusing flock of sheep.

'I'm used to driving myself around London, Jared, and I took my licence there, though I must admit I met few sheep, but thanks for the compliment. It's a great concession on your part.'

That night Emma sat at her dining-room table in solitary state.

'Why Baas Jared eat outside?' Rosie demanded.

'He wants to,' said Emma coldly.

She had told Rosie she would eat a boiled egg and bread and butter for supper – and Rosie had served it in a silver holder on a silver platter and with a silver egg cutter to complete the picture. It looks ridiculous, Emma decided, but she had only herself to blame, for she had told Rosie they should make use of the family heirlooms.

From outside came the savoury haunting fragrance of meat grilled on the open coals. Jared had disappeared into the butcher's on the way home and must have purchased lamb chops and boerewors, the beef sausage, spiced with herbs, that was so delicious cooked in this way.

Emma wandered restlessly around the house until Rosie called to tell her she had put her coffee on the stoep. When she came to get it she noticed the old servant had put two cups on the tray. Emma could see a glowing fire across the yard and the dark figure of Jared bending over it, and against her will, she was impelled to go towards him. Think of a reason quickly, she told herself.

'I was wondering, Jared, whether you have any textbooks about farming to lend to me,' she asked him.

He looked up, tossing back a lock of dark hair that had fallen over his eyes. His brown skin was ruddy in the light of the fire.

'Yes, of course, Emma. But hang on while I finish cooking this meat.'

'I didn't intend you should eat alone. Rosie is livid.'

'Only that I should sleep alone, is that it?'

Emma did not reply.

'This looks good, doesn't it?' he went on.

'It smells out of this world,' said Emma.

'What did Rosie cook for you tonight?'

'A boiled egg.'

'What? Oh, for God's sake, Emma, I didn't think you were the kind of woman to sit down to a boiled egg the moment you found yourself alone. If you're going to do that, I'll have to come in for some meals, I can see that.'

'I think Rosie would like it,' said Emma.

'And of course we must keep her happy, mustn't we?' grinned Jared. 'And meanwhile, how about sharing this braai and I'll have some of your coffee?'

Emma went back to fetch the tray.

'Dare I ask you to come into the museum?' said Jared. 'The south-easter has arrived and it will be cold on the stoep. In any case, when we've eaten, I must find those books for you.'

The museum looked better now it had been cleaned. A lamp on a small table cast a golden glow that did not reach up to the shadowy beams of the roof. Emma sat opposite Jared at the plain deal table and ate chops and sausages with her fingers from a tin plate, wiping her hands with a paper towel when she had finished.

'That was very good,' she admitted.

'You have a healthier appetite than Yolande, in spite of the fact that you're much thinner than she,' he said. 'It must be your redheaded temperament that burns up the calories.'

'I'm not thin,' Emma protested.

She felt his eyes on her and was conscious that her shirt was casually unbuttoned and probably showed more of her breasts than she would have chosen to show if she had thought she was going to come over here to be with Jared. Too late now to worry about that. She was not a teenager to appear embarrassed by a man's interested scrutiny.

'No, Emma, you're not thin. You have a very alluring appearance – as I think I must have told you before.'

She glanced up and met the dark gaze of his brilliant eyes.

'I think I'd better take those books and go, Jared, if I'm to study them tonight.'

'How about the coffee you offered me?' he said, ignoring her remark. 'I have some beautiful old brandy here. You must try a little. It will warm you before you venture out again into the cold wind.'

He poured a little into a balloon goblet and went to sit on the bed.

'Sorry I haven't any easy chairs, Emma. You can't drink brandy sitting on a wooden stool. Come over here and sit beside me.'

He patted the bed encouragingly and she found herself walking as if hypnotized towards him.

'Cup it in your hands and soon you'll be able to breathe the fumes. It's a very civilized way of drinking, don't you think?'

'I don't know,' she said. 'I've never tried it before.'

She sat beside him very conscious that she was behaving foolishly and that the longer she stayed the more difficult it would be to tear herself away. And yet she could not go. The brandy became alive in her warm hands and she imitated him, inhaling the breathtaking aroma and feeling that without taking one sip the very fragrance of it was rushing to her head.

'Sip a little,' he encouraged her, and she cautiously did so. A flash of golden fire seemed to go like lightning into her being, producing a fantastic glow. She wanted to set it aside, and yet she went on holding the warm aromatic glass. An idea had occurred to her. Suppose she told Mr. Johnson that Jared had invited her into his room and plied her with brandy, would that constitute unsuitable behaviour? She took another sip and again the golden glow filtered down, giving her a feeling of wellbeing. Was it a good idea? she wondered. In this day and age a girl could hardly complain that she had been lured into doing something against her will. She was supposed to be a modern woman who could take care of herself. However, she must try to get rid of Jared by some means. Perhaps Mr. Johnson would believe her, for after all, he was quite an old-fashioned person.

'Don't drink it too quickly,' Jared warned her. 'You're supposed to savour it. I don't want to have to carry you back.'

She set her glass aside and stretched herself out on the bed.

'I feel wonderful,' she said. 'All glowing and warm and completely relaxed. It was horrible of me to say I disliked you, Jared. Let's kiss and be friends.'

He leaned over her, putting his hands on both sides of her, and she gazed up into his eyes that were quizzical, examining her closely.

'This is a sudden change, Emma. It couldn't be that you're trying to put something across on me, could it?'

'What do you mean? How could I be doing that?' she asked.

'Just putting two and two together and multiplying it into a frame-up. You told me Mr. Johnson told you you could maybe get rid of me if I behaved badly, and maybe making love to you on my bed after giving you brandy might be considered a good reason.'

Emma opened her dark blue eyes wide. How could he be so perceptive? His face was very close to hers, the dark eyes inscrutable, the mouth firm and arrogant, a little cruel.

'How could you think I would do such a think?' she said innocently.

'I think you're a very determined young lady, Emma, set on getting your own way. But I warn you, don't start any tricks, because two can play at your game. You've asked me for a kiss and you're going to get it.'

She felt the hard weight of him and then he was kissing her roughly and passionately. She missed the gentleness she had sensed in him before. With one hand he was holding her down firmly and his other hand was seeking the open shirt front as his mouth continued the kiss. She pulled herself from his grasp and stood up shakily. They stared at each other and again she thought that his eyes were like the glowing coals seen when a wild animal is encountered unexpectedly in the light of headlamps.

'So you've had enough already?' he demanded, using a tone of voice she had never heard before, sneering at her weakness. 'Let this be a lesson to you, Emma. Don't start anything you don't mean to continue. Now take your textbooks and go. I've had enough of women and their ways for one day!'

CHAPTER SIX

As the weeks passed, the weather became hotter and it was no longer pleasant to sit on the open verandah. The table was drawn back into the dappled shade of the old vine whose leaves were dark green now with sprays of grapes that were hard and small at first but began to grow plumper by the day, encouraged by the dazzling heat of the constant sun.

Not that there was much time for sitting outside, but in the morning Emma took her breakfast there, enjoying the iced papaya and Rosie's fresh *mosbolletjies*, a kind of bread roll, hot and fragrant. Since the episode when she had shared his supper, Jared had withdrawn from her and seemed quite indifferent. All the same, they were constantly in each other's company, for he kept his word to her uncle and seemed determined to train her to look after the farm. She wondered whether this was because he expected to leave soon.

Day after day she accompanied him on his rounds, inspecting the new crop for the insects and pests which were liable to attack the young trees, or helping with the fertilization that had to be carried out all the time. She had begun to realize that she could not have managed without his help, but each day she felt she was gaining knowledge and some day she hoped she would be able to do it on her own. The citrus industry was highly organized and had a research station in the district and a staff of field officers who lived in the area and visited growers to advise them on the care of their trees, so Emma felt that even if Jared did leave she would not be entirely helpless.

This morning Jared had come from the lands while she

was still breakfasting.

'I'm almost ready,' she told him. 'Won't you have some coffee?'

'Too hot,' he said. 'I'll get some water from Rosie in the kitchen.'

He came back later clinking the ice in his glass.

'It's going to be another scorcher. It seems too bad to make you come out in it. You look so cool.'

She was dressed in pale lime yellow shorts with a matching top, sleeveless and cut low with a scooped neck. Her skin was matt, unlike most redheads, and she was acquiring an even golden tan.

'Do you think it's all right for me to wear shorts around the farm?' she asked. 'It's so hot to wear jeans now.'

He looked at her, his eyes sweeping her from top to toe.

'Why not?' he said indifferently. 'I wear shorts myself, and we mustn't forget that you're a free woman, must we?'

She found she hated his coldness and longed for the old teasing compliments. He must be saving those for Yolande – goodness knows, he met her often enough. She stole a glance at him and wondered how she could still find his looks so attractive when his whole attitude was utterly frigid towards her. He had taken off the wide-brimmed hat and his hair was over his forehead in damp curls, making him look almost boyish. His thin cotton shirt was open to the waist showing the golden glow of his skin and the soft dark curls on his chest. In shorts, his legs looked long and lithe, not barrel-shaped like most of her farming friends.

And that reminded her that she was going to see Terry again tonight. Since that first time they had gone out together, he had been a persistent suitor, doggedly keeping on asking for her company in spite of some attempts she had made to avoid him.

'I've only just arrived here,' she had protested when he kept asking her to accompany him to various functions. 'I don't want to date the same person all the time.'

He had smiled his slow good-natured smile and agreed that as she was a newcomer she should be allowed to play the field as he put it. And then the very next day he phoned again asking for another date.

'Your large lover is on the line again,' Jared had told her.

'Why do you sneer at Terry? He's tall and good-looking and awfully kind and good-natured.'

'You mean he's not very interesting.'

'No, of course I don't!' she snapped. 'He's quite good company. You make me furious when you assume that a man can't be interesting to a woman if he's solid and nice.'

'It sounds as if you've found him safe enough,' Jared commented.

'Yes, I have. Not like others I could mention.'

'Beautiful Emma, it's worth aggravating you a bit to see that pink flower in your cheeks and the gorgeous contrast of those indignant blue eyes. Believe me, you'll soon tire of your solid citizen,' he assured her.

But this conversation had taken place some while ago when he was still paying her compliments. Lately Jared had treated her with such coolness that she had continued to see Terry to bolster her pride. She needed to feel that she was still charming to someone. And Terry was so safe – perhaps a little too safe. Not in the least exciting. But she liked his family. He came from a great sprawling farm with various houses where they all lived, father, mother, grandparents, aunts, brothers, sisters, married relatives and the younger generation. It was quite bewildering.

He had asked her to spend Christmas Day with them and soon she would have to make up her mind whether to accept his invitation. What had made her hesitate? She supposed it was the fact that she had wanted to spend her first South African Christmas in her own home. But that was foolish, she knew, for who would be here?

Not Jared, certainly, for he was sure to go to Heron's Creek for the day to be with Yolande. She wanted to ask Jared what his plans were and yet did not want to appear curious or make him think she expected him to stay here. Though why she was worrying about this she did not know, for Jared would do exactly as he pleased whatever the circumstances.

Today they were using a small four-wheel-drive vehicle that had an awning over the top to provide shade. There was little room between the small bucket seats and their warm limbs brushed each other as they drove along, but only Emma seemed conscious of it and Jared looked straight ahead. The blossom had gone now and the oranges were green upon the darker green of the leafy trees.

'I've been reading your books and they are very factual,' Emma remarked to Jared, 'but they don't tell you anything about how oranges came here or where they came from in the first place.'

They were standing at a safe distance, watching a large complicated-looking vehicle spraying the young trees with some kind of pesticide.

'You seem to have a positive lust for information that's in no way useful to you at the moment,' Jared remarked. 'I would have thought it was better to concentrate on the more practical aspects. But if you must know, they came from places like India, Malaya and Cochin-China.'

'I love that name!' she smiled. 'It sounds so romantic.'

'Glad you find some romance in the industry. All I can think of at the moment are the problems, scale and fruit flies and red spider and citrus aphis and mealy bug.'

'I hate having to use insecticides,' said Emma. 'Isn't there any other method?'

'These days you have to use some modern methods,' he told her, 'but we do try to encourage ladybirds and parasitic wasps because they're natural enemies of some of the harmful insects.'

He put his hand on her arm to move her further away from the approaching sprayer. Why did she always feel this vibrant thrill when Jared touched her? Even when Terry kissed her good night it was like kissing a brother. She looked up at him, at his dark hair blowing free in the warm breeze, his dark eyes intent upon the spraying of the orchard, the curving firmness of his lips. Why, oh, why did she feel this intense physical attraction that had nothing to do with the man's fierce character, the kind of arrogant nature that she so disliked? Yolande would think her crazy to be discussing insect pests with him. And for the last few weeks they had exchanged hardly a word that was not based on the practical running of the farm.

'When did they start growing citrus fruit in this country?' she persisted.

'Way back,' said Jared, 'before we even became a colony, the Dutch East India settlers sent the sailing ship *Tulp* to St. Helena to bring back various fruits including citrus. But the orange industry really began in this district in about 1854 when a Mr. Tuck of Grahamstown began to distribute navel orange trees propagated by budding.'

'Isn't that the same method we use now?'

'Right first time. We plant seeds from the rough skin type of lemon, then when they're established a bud of a variety of orange, say the navel or Valencia, is cut from the parent tree and inserted under the bark. When this has formed a strong shoot the top of the lemon seedling is cut away. Then about twelve months later, the young tree made up of the rough lemon roots and the navel or Valencia top is ready to be planted in the orchard.'

'And when does it bear fruit?'

'About five or six years later, and it stays of value until it's about forty years old, with ten to twenty-five years of age as the best period. You see, an orange tree is like a

93

woman, give or take a few years.'

She looked up at him. His dark eyes were regarding her steadily. There was something mysterious and impenetrable about his expression. All thoughts of his lecture flew from her mind, and she tried desperately to grasp at something that would restore the practical aspect of their conversation.

'What happens about the picking and packing?'

'You'll find out all about that when the time comes. Meanwhile say a prayer that we get no heavy storms or hail. We're not in the hail belt, we hope, but it has been known to come and devastate a whole crop.'

His eyes seemed gentler now. He was looking more friendly than he had done for some time.

'If you're so interested,' he went on, 'I can bring some other books across this evening and discuss them with you.'

'I'm sorry, it will have to be some other time. I have promised Terry I would go out with him.'

His expression hardened again.

'Too bad. I suppose you'll be spending Christmas Day with Terry too.'

'He's asked me,' she admitted, 'but I haven't accepted yet.'

'That's fine as far as I'm concerned. It will be interesting for you to have a real South African farm Christmas with such a large family. The problem around Christmas time is that our labour force usually gets drunk or just doesn't turn up, and you have to watch that the cattle don't suffer and that the hens get fed, but I can see to that before I go to Heron's Creek.'

So he was going, and she would not be spending Christmas with him. It had been foolish of her to think she might. And of course it was the last thing she wanted to do, she assured herself. She would be far happier with Terry's large family.

She spent one of those pleasant, slightly boring evenings with Terry having dinner at the small hotel and seeing a three-year-old Western that she would never have chosen to go to in London even if it had been new. She listened passively to Terry's descriptions, very detailed, of the exploits of his hunting dog and the merits of his different guns. On the way home she drowsed, for she had had a long day around the farm with Jared. Her head drooped on to Terry's shoulder and he put one arm around her as his automatic gears took charge on the rather bumpy road. She was jerked awake by his sudden exclamation.

'What the devil . . .? Did you see that?'

'What was it, Terry?'

Emma sat up straight, discarding the weight of his arm from her shoulder.

'I could have sworn it was a leopard!' he exclaimed.

'A leopard? But surely there are none left in this part of the country?'

'I saw it only for a moment in the headlights. But it was too big for a civet, far too big, a full-grown animal, I would say.'

Emma glanced behind her rather fearfully. The country lay all around them, dark and bushy with not a light to be seen.

'Do you want to go back?' she asked.

'No, of course not. What could we do? I haven't even got a gun with me. In any case, if it was a leopard, they're protected. I'd never think of shooting one. But what an incredible thing! It's very near to Sunglow. You'd better tell Jared – you don't want to lose any of those Brahmin cows that the old man took such a pride in.'

Emma could not help wondering whether Terry really had seen a leopard. He had not got much imagination otherwise, but when it came to hunting, she thought he would have been prepared to believe there were lions on

95

the farm. Jared would probably scoff at the whole idea.

There was a light in the museum room when they got back.

'Old Jared is still up. Shall we go and tell him?' asked Terry.

'No, I will,' Emma replied. 'I'll tell him tomorrow.'

She feared that Jared might be too caustic if Terry arrived at this time of night with such a tall tale. She got rid of Terry quite soon with the excuse that they had both to be up at dawn tomorrow and went to bed. But she could not sleep. In spite of her scepticism about Terry's leopard, she began to wonder what he had seen. Life went on in such a domestic fashion here that one was inclined to forget that one was in Africa, and surrounded by hundreds of miles of wild country. Eventually she firmly banished it from her mind and appreciatively shrugging down under a sheet and one blanket she fell asleep.

Just as she thought would happen, Jared scoffed at the idea of Terry's having seen a leopard.

'What did you give your fat friend to drink?' he asked. 'Do you know, Emma, there can't have been a leopard around here for at least fifty years. He was just trying to impress you. He knows all English people think there'll be lions walking in the streets of Johannesburg. He probably saw a large species of wild cat. You know how crazy he is about hunting.'

'Well, I'm glad you think so, Jared,' Emma said calmly. 'But Terry said I was to tell you to watch Uncle Mac's Brahmin calves.'

'They're your Brahmin calves now, and they're perfectly safe. They get locked up in the kraal each night. What do you suggest we should do, build a boma for them?'

'What's a kraal, and what's a boma?' asked Emma.

'Good God, girl, you should be ashamed of your ignorance! A kraal is a place for cattle guarded by a low stone wall and a gate where they get herded at night, and a boma is an extra protection around it built of thorny bush. But I don't think we've come to that yet.'

Emma made a special expedition to inspect her Brahmins. There were only a few of them, beautiful animals with their dark humps and their creamy pelts, their loose, almost scalloped frill of a dewlap and their gentle eyes. The little calves were miniatures of their handsome father. Emma was glad that Jared had scorned the idea of a leopard in the vicinity.

It was odd to think that Christmas was approaching, but with none of the usual accompaniments of snow or colder weather or log fires. Instead the weather became hotter by the day. To grow properly, oranges need hot summer days and cool winter nights to colour up the fruit, and at this time of the year they were certainly getting their share of heat in the hot dry valleys. It looked strange in the shops to see artificial holly and Christmas tree decorations, and the cards had been on sale since September. Emma had purchased cards and calendars with exotic African scenes for her friends overseas and had posted them in early November, but now she bought a few suitable presents for Terry's relatives, preserved fruits and imported chocolates.

But what was she to do about Jared? They were in such intimate contact all day long, yet should they exchange presents? He had been so cool towards her for weeks that she could not imagine that he would think about giving her anything. And yet he did so much for her on the farm that she felt she should give him some token. How difficult it all was! On Christmas Eve she bought a bottle of Courvoisier brandy and a book on tribal costume, spending far more money than she could really afford, but she felt she must buy Jared something luxurious or else nothing at all. Having finished shopping for presents, she decided she must have a new dress for Christmas Day and investigated the local dress shops until she found a light cool cotton of medium length in a pretty print of brown, orange and white, with a feminine look, frilled at the hem and with a corresponding frill on its scooped neckline. It looked festive yet practical. She invested in a brief yellow bikini because Terry had told her they would spend part of the day beside the large swimming pool on his farm.

She went into the toy department of the one large store in the little town and bought tinsel and decorations, thinking she would find a small real tree on the farm, and she saw with sympathy that, even in this stifling climate, there was a Father Christmas, dressed as if he had come from the North Pole, complete with massive white beard and wig and huge boots, distributing parcels and cool drinks and sweets to little children clad only in brief shorts.

Getting out of the small car laden with parcels, Emma met Jared crossing the yard.

'You're taking Christmas seriously,' he said. 'I usually try to ignore it as far as possible.'

When he had helped her to carry the parcels in, she asked him to have a beer.

'Is there a small tree I could have?' she said.

'But why bother?' he asked. 'Or are you intending to do some entertaining?'

'No, but I just feel it would be good to look a bit festive. After all, it is my first Christmas here.'

'And you're spending it with Terry.'

She wanted to say, whose fault is that? If he had not been going to Yolande's place she would have stayed at home herself.

'Will you be in this evening?'

She nodded.

'All right, I'll see what I can find for you and bring it over.'

'Come for dinner,' she invited. 'Rosie is cooking a leg of lamb and I won't be able to eat much of it. But they're having two days off, so I can exist for the rest of the holiday on cold meat and salad.'

She expected him to say that he was going out with Yolande, but instead he accepted. 'I'll be there.'

How ridiculous it was! Emma felt in as much of a flutter as she had felt all those years ago when he had said he would come to the dance with her. What should she wear? If she wore the new dress, it would seem to be making too much of an occasion, and besides, she must save it for tomorrow. She would wear a flip skirt of dark avocado green with a lighter green cotton blouse, cool and sleeveless, and a narrow belt of green webbing. It emphasized the colour of her hair and the light golden tan she had acquired since she came here.

She told Rosie that Jared would be coming to dinner and the old African maid was most approving.

'I must do roast potatoes now, Miss Emma, instead of the new ones you ordered. Baas Jared he always say to me "Rosie, no one roasts potatoes like you. They're out of the world," and I will open a new jar of redcurrant jelly and make mint sauce and there are some new small peas that I got in special for tonight. What about pudding?'

'Oh, Rosie, I don't think you need bother about pudding. We can have fruit and cheese and biscuits.'

'No bother. I will make Baas Jared's special, fruit salad with fresh pineapple, peaches and white wine. How would you like that? Now, Miss Emma, you go and make yourself pretty.'

She hustled off to give orders to the Umfaan, a young African boy who helped her in the kitchen.

I'm a fool, Emma told herself, winding her glowing hair around her head and twisting the little side pieces until they hung on each side of her face in spiralling curls. She put on fine tights and high-heeled shoes for a change and used some of the French perfume she had bought duty-free on the plane. What am I doing, making myself beautiful for this man who doesn't even like me and runs to Yolande all the time? she thought. And I don't like him either – I've told him so. What's happened to my plans to be rid of him? Oh, stupid, stupid, stupid! she told her reflection in the mirror. But the face looked back at her with sparkling eyes and soft rose-coloured lips and a smile that spilled over with excitement.

Jared arrived at seven, bringing with him a small thorn tree, its roots buried in a pot of red earth, its leaves young and emerald green and its spiky silver thorns presenting perfect places to hang baubles.

'Not exactly in tradition,' he admitted, grinning. 'But it was all I could find.'

'It's a nice shape,' she answered.

'Yes, isn't it?' he said. She looked up at him and he was not looking at the tree. She felt herself blushing.

'Let's put it near the hearth and I'll decorate it now,' she suggested.

'I'll give this champagne to Rosie to put in the ice bucket,' said Jared.

He went into the kitchen and she could hear him laughing with Rosie. She kneeled beside the tree, arranging the glittering gay ornaments and the silver tinsel. She had saved the angel for the top and was just fixing it when she heard his voice from the doorway.

'Why do angels never have red hair, I wonder?'

'I suppose because redheaded people are seldom angelic.'

'No, no, they're too temperamental to make good angels, aren't they?'

'I haven't noticed any dark-haired angels either,' she retorted.

'Mm, yes, but the devil is always portrayed with dark eyes and hair, isn't he?'

'Of course,' she said, looking up at him.

In the glow of the lamps, his colouring looked even darker than usual and certainly he could have sat for a portrait of Lucifer, she thought, black-haired, black-eyed, proud and arrogant. She felt a quiver of fear. Had she been wise to break down the reserve that had existed between them during the last few weeks? But it's Christmas, she excused herself. And I'm not to be with him tomorrow. Why shouldn't I have dinner with him? It will only be for a couple of hours. And tomorrow I'll hardly see him at all.

'Why are you kneeling there concentrating so earnestly?' he asked.

'Just wondering whether it has enough decorations now.'

'It looks good to me,' he said.

He was looking down at her as she kneeled upon the sheepskin rug in front of the hearth and he was looking at her, not the tree. He put out his hands and lifted her to her feet.

'Let's bury our differences on Christmas Eve, shall we?'

The ornaments on the little tree winked and quivered in the lamplight.

'It seems symbolic somehow to have a thorn tree instead of a northern fir,' said Emma. 'This is such a country of thorn trees. They look so dry, just brittle silver in the winter, but by summertime I always thought they looked like blossoming gold with all those fluffy sprays of flowers on them.'

'I nipped some of the thorns off before I brought it to you, Emma,' he said, 'perhaps that's symbolic too.'

'What do you mean?' she asked.

'I mean that on Christmas Eve I'll try to be as circumspect as my mistress desires, but she must try to be less prickly.'

He was still holding her hands and it seemed to her as if

she were grasping a dynamo that was sending flashes of magnetic fire though her whole body. She resisted the desire to wrench her hands away, but dropped them slowly, saying, 'Shall we have our drink on the patio? You haven't seen that I've had the old swing seat recovered. It came back today. That's my Christmas present to the house.'

However, when she was seated beside him on the yellow and white striped seat with its sheltering awning, she thought that perhaps she had been unwise to come out here with him. It was so voluptuous, sinking into the soft cushions and drinking the chilled golden sparkling wine in the blue hazy darkness. She felt happy and relaxed and off her guard, and she was glad when Rosie rang the bell to indicate that they must come in to dinner.

The meal was a success. Rosie had prepared a starter of eggs and anchovies with her homemade mayonnaise and decorated it with stuffed olives. This was followed by delicious lamb with small peas and potatoes that could not have been more golden or more crisp. The peaches in white wine rounded off the meal and when they had finished, Rosie announced that she had put coffee and liqueurs outside on the patio.

'I like your seat, Emma,' said Jared. 'It has a sensuous charm that appeals to me.'

Rosie had taken the tray away and said good night, and now Emma was conscious that she was alone with him, and that it would be dangerous to stay here, for she was too conscious of this man, too aware that he had only to touch her and her whole self longed to surrender to his will. From the African quarters far away on the farm there came singing and the strumming of a guitar, bittersweet with sensuous desire.

She leaned back on the soft cushions and felt his arm that had been along the back of the seat touching her, stroking her upper arms so that she was aware of their satiny smooth texture beneath his fingers. She sat still, not wanting to stop him but assuring herself that at any moment she could. She felt unwilling to deny the breathless emotion that was coursing through her body, and yet tried to tell herself that if she willed it she could break this almost hypnotic spell that she sensed when he was beside her. Then his hand curved around the nape of her neck and he was holding her so that she was forced to encounter his dark, mysterious expression, only dimly perceived in the shadow of the canopy. She closed her eyes, and felt his fingers tracing the curve of her throat, then upwards to her mouth where they outlined its shape, so soft and vulnerable

And then he was kissing her, a slow languorous kiss, that was at one with the slow beat of the guitar, the throbbing sound of the cicadas echoing in vibrant harmony across the still warm night. His arms were round her now and her hand came up to caress his face. She felt her lips part under his and the kiss which had begun so gently became hard and fiercely passionate. When it was over she did not give him time to speak but tore herself from his arms and almost ran towards the glass door that led into the living-room, for she felt she must get away from him before he spoiled the radiance of her experience with words. She feared whatever he might say, for she knew how badly he could wound her. But he swiftly crossed the paving that was still warm from the heat of the day and before she could find refuge he had caught her up against the muscular hardness of his body. She dared not turn or look at him, for she felt she could not meet his eyes since her own would betray her.

'Why are you running away from me?' he demanded.

'Please let me go, Jared,' she whispered.

He still held her closely and she knew the weakness of sensual desire. She felt his face close against her own brushing her cheek with his lips.

'Lovely Emma, try to deny now that you feel some passion for me. Try to say that you feel no stirring of the senses when we kiss.'

She turned towards him now, but evaded his arms.

'Why should I deny it? You're certainly an expert at making a girl feel desired and desirous. But I'm under no illusions about you. I know it comes from long years of experience. When I give my love to someone, it will not be a man like you, who thinks of all women as sexual objects, who takes pride in being able to charm any number. No, Jared, I don't deny your sensual attraction, but I need someone who isn't attracted by every pretty face he sees.'

A frown darkened his expression.

'So that's your opinion of me, is it? Too bad! From your description of your ideal man it seems as if Terry Owen might stand a chance after all.'

'Who knows?' said Emma. 'Good night, Jared.'

'Good night, my lovely Emma. I broke my word to you and I guess I got what I deserved. You're a hard task-master, aren't you? I'll wish you a happy Christmas in the morning. You invited me to breakfast and I'm still holding you to that. Who knows, perhaps it might rate a kiss, since they seem to be handed out only on very special occasions.'

He was incorrigible and utterly without scruples where women were concerned. Her mind fought against him – and yet her physical self thrilled to each casual caress.

CHAPTER SEVEN

Emma lay awake for a long time, hearing the sensuous throbbing of the guitar in the warm African night. When she thought of their kiss, her body trembled – and yet she felt she had been wise to repudiate him. But the emotional side of her nature was like a child waiting for Christmas morning. They would meet at breakfast, for Jared had said he would come before they each went their different ways.

Suppose he kissed her then and suggested they should spend the day together? Oh, then she could believe he was more serious than she had thought. If he were to say they would go up into the mountains or to the forest she would be compelled to make some excuse to Terry, for she knew she desired to be with Jared with all her heart. She imagined them driving up into the cool forest, being alone with the scent of pine needles all around them. She was foolish to dream of such a thing. It would never happen, and if it did, what then? She longed to be with him, and yet she knew it was dangerous to feel like this, for with him she felt a passionate desire that demanded fulfilment. But if he asked her, could she refuse?

She woke early and dressed in her new dress, so feminine with its frills at hem and neck, emphasizing the rounded curves of her breasts and the satin smoothness of her brown arms. She knotted her hair in an upward sweep, for the day promised heat, though at this hour everything smelled fragrant, fresh and cool. She could smell the grass where it had been mown the day before and the scent of the white-flowering jasmine below on the porch.

Rosie was in the kitchen with an apron over her best

black satin dress, delighted with the black shawl that Emma had given her. She was to go as soon as breakfast was finished.

'We'll have it outside, Rosie,' she decided. 'We don't need much, just orange juice, scrambled eggs and coffee and toast, I think.'

'I have set the table out there on the stoep, Miss Emma, but Baas Jared sent a note across with one of the picca-nins. I left it there for you.'

Emma went slowly out to the stoep and looked at the note. Jared's bold hand had written 'Emma' across the folded paper. Her hand trembled a little as she reached for it, for she had a premonition that she would not be pleased with its contents.

'Emma, I've had a call to go to Heron's Creek earlier than I expected. I've organized the staff, but I'll be back in the afternoon to see to the chores. Meanwhile enjoy your day with Terry and a happy Christmas. Sorry I couldn't wish it in person.'

Why had he left and gone to Yolande's place so early? Was he trying to avoid meeting her? Had he had second thoughts about his amorous behaviour last night? But no, he was not the kind to regret that. Emma felt hurt and humiliated. Had he taken the easy way out by going off to Yolande because he thought she herself would expect a follow-up to their intimate scene? Or had he been more deeply offended than she thought when she had repudi-ated his lovemaking? No, the simple explanation was probably the true one – that last night he had been amus-ing himself because he had nothing else to do, just as five years ago he had amused himself with an Emma much younger and more vulnerable.

But I'm vulnerable now, thought Emma, sitting at the table and looking through a mist of tears at the small Swedish ornament of revolving gilt angels that she had told Rosie to place there as a centrepiece. What a fool I was to ask him to dinner last night! I wish I'd kept him at a distance rather than end by feeling so snubbed and deserted this morning.

The phone rang and she rushed towards it thinking it might be Jared. But it was Terry asking if he could come and fetch her.

'No, Terry, I'll drive myself,' she said.

She wanted to be able to get away at any time she chose, so she would take her own small car. It was the first time she had had to lock the door of the house from outside, but Rosie and her helpers would be away for the day. She knew that Jared had a key if he needed to get in before she came home. She put her presents, gaily wrapped and beribboned, into the little car, and remembered to include her bikini and a beach towel in case they bathed, but she did not feel very festive.

Why should she feel so flat and let down? It was her own fault that she had invited Jared to dinner, and if she had had any sense she would have known what the consequence would be. Put the thought of him behind you, she told herself. He's rushed off to Yolande and didn't even bother to come to breakfast with you or wish you a happy Christmas as he promised. So why worry? You're going to spend your first South African Christmas with a congenial family at a luxurious farm. And Terry will be sweet and kind to you and not bewilder you with passionate lovemaking only to let you down. She held on to the idea of Terry, trying to dismiss Jared from her mind, but his dark face was imprinted too clearly in her memory as she drove carefully through the farmlands distributing lollipops to small Africans, who ran towards each gate to open it, shouting 'Chlissmas box!' with hopeful wide white-toothed smiles.

Behind the small car, there was a constant stream of dry red dust that settled upon the tall corn growing nearest to the road. In the distance, the mountains were already shimmering with a misty pink colour from the heat. It seemed all so unlikely for Christmas Day. Last year Emma had gone with her mother to a hotel in the Lake District and they had skated on the frozen water amidst hills covered with snow.

A bewildering assortment of Terry's relations greeted her from the spacious covered patio at the front of the large house. They were having morning tea and a succession of trolleys brought forward by maids in floral dresses and floral headgear disclosed large teapots, coffee pots, and plates of every kind of cake, cream scones, savoury scones, sandwiches and koeksusters dripping with syrup. Old aunts sat in the shade chattering as if they had not seen each other for months, though Emma knew they saw each other practically every day. An assortment of young children played in the sun on swings and seesaws, and the older ones came in now and then from the tennis court or burst dripping upon the scene to claim a plate of cakes to take for their friends at the swimming bath.

Emma was introduced to the people she had not yet met as 'Terry's girl-friend.' Everyone was very friendly and interested in her. Terry's grandmother patted the seat beside her.

'Come and see me before you dash off with Terry to have a swim. Have another koeksuster. With your figure you can afford it, and I can too, for I don't have to worry any more.'

She was plump, rosy, and a comfortable-looking old lady with silver hair and bright blue eyes.

'How are you getting on with Jared Wells?' she went on. 'I believe old Mac left him as your manager. Why didn't you bring him along today? I adore him. I think he's the most exciting man in the district.'

'He's gone to Heron's Creek to spend Christmas with the Mitchells,' Emma told her.

'Oh, yes, I understand the daughter is very attractive.

Well, it's about time Jared settled down, and they have money too, I believe. Good thing for Terry's sake that he's interested in that direction, my dear, for you're very lovely yourself. I expect Jared has told you so. He's always been a devil for charming women, young and old, but not as old as me, unfortunately. Whoever gets him will have to hang on to him, for he's a sly one.'

'Gran, let me see something of Emma,' Terry put in. 'You can't have her all the time! I want to take her for a swim. We must get up an appetite for that turkey.'

It was pleasant to feel popular and wanted, thought Emma. She changed into her new bright yellow bikini and received many wolf whistles from the crowd of young people by the pool.

'You look great,' Terry told her.

He always said this. In her mind she heard the echo of a low thrilling voice, 'Lovely golden Emma, you can't know how utterly beautiful you look.'

She swam in the pale green pool with its fountain at one end and its mosaic of a mermaid upon the bottom that seemed to move under the waves as if alive. All around there were sweeping green lawns, well watered by irrigation from the farm's dam, and a lovely rose garden with lavender bushes wafting their sweet scent across the grass. It was incredible that all this could exist beside the dry bushy country through which she had driven this morning. Anyone who married Terry would have a beautiful ready-made home, but they would have to be sociable, for the family seemed all closely bound together, though aparently all very good-natured and willing to let her, a stranger, in.

She watched Terry playing with his young cousins, ducking them and being splashed in his turn. He was so sensible and kind, she thought. Why then was her mind constantly drawn to that other farm to wonder what Jared was doing?

Lunch was served on a long table under the oak trees in front of the house. It seemed crazy to be eating so much in the heat of the day, although most of it was cold. However, there was a flaming Christmas pudding, served with brandy butter, and fast melting ice cream, and everyone was delighted when Emma was the one to find a ring in her portion.

All morning behind the mountains white cumulus clouds had been showing their swelling tops as if they were monsters waiting to take over the scene, and now they began to tower overhead and threatened to blot out the radiant sun.

'The weather looks dicey. I'd better go to see that the cattle are in their kraal,' Terry said, releasing Emma's hand from under the table.

'Can I come too?' she asked.

When she got out into the open farmlands, she saw that the weather looked very threatening indeed.

'I wonder whether I should make for home?' she asked.

'Not yet, Emma. Stay a bit longer. Jared will be there to see to things, won't he?'

'I'm not sure. I suppose so,' said Emma doubtfully.

'He's your manager, it's up to him to see that things are in order. Surely you trust him?'

Do I? thought Emma. Perhaps I do trust him to run the farm, but not in anything else.

The white of the cumulus clouds had changed now to a gloomy grey and the two of them had to struggle against the strong south-west wind as they hurried to the cattle sheds. Emma helped to batten things down, see that the stable doors were closed and the cattle protected from the weather.

'You'd make a good farmer's wife,' Terry laughed. He put his arm around her to protect her from the wind and it was as if a brother were touching her, kind and unexciting.

'I think I'll phone when we get back to the house,' said Emma. She felt uneasy that Sunglow was possibly neglected in the storm, but surely Jared would be there?

It was incredible how quickly the weather had changed. The black clouds were scudding across the sky and they could hardly keep their feet against the force of the wind, as they struggled back to the house.

'Will a storm be bad for the orange harvest?' gasped Emma.

'Could be,' answered Terry laconically. 'Depends where it strikes.'

Lights were on in the house and the whole place looked glowing with welcome and noise, the Christmas tree in the living-room strung with coloured lights, the small children playing with cars in the wide passage, the older ones hard at their table tennis in the games room, others dancing to the record player. Someone had rigged up a projector and the older relatives were watching a film.

Emma could get no response from the house or the museum, where there was an extension.

'It's hardly likely you would, is it?' said Terry sensibly. 'Jared is probably out seeing to the cattle.'

By now jagged streaks of lightning were flashing across the sky.

'I must go, Terry,' Emma insisted. She knew she would not feel happy until she was back at Sunglow.

'I can't let you go on your own. I'll come with you.'

'No, no, I don't want you to. You may be needed here. It's only a little distance, I'll be quite all right.'

She was quite determined to go, and overcame all their protests. The rain had not quite started yet and she hoped to get home before the storm broke properly. But on the road the little car bucked and jumped like an erratic horse as the gusts of wind caught it and made it veer from its path. She drove slowly and carefully, but before she had gone far, great blobs of rain splashed across the windscreen and soon the red dust was a sea of mud in which the car slithered and skidded. Sometimes she could not see an inch in front of her, but fortunately there was no other traffic on the road. However, stray sheep and cows gave her a fright every now and again as they loomed up in the light of the headlamps, that she had turned on although it was only late afternoon.

In the morning it had taken her twenty minutes to get to Terry's farm, but now she had been three-quarters of an hour on the road and she still had to cross the causeway where there was only a low roadway across the river. There was a steep drop to this and fortunately she braked to find out how best to negotiate it. She could hardly believe her eyes. Earlier in the day she had crossed with ease across the dry roadway with its foot-high curbs. There had been only flat rocks and sandy red soil and here and there a small pool of water. But now the causeway was covered, and the river was coming down swiftly, wide and quite deep. Would she be able to cross?

She got out of the car and tested the depth with a stick that she found nearby. It was a foot deep at the edge. Surely her little car could negotiate this? Slowly and cautiously she edged her way into the stream. She was on the causeway, but the water was swifter than she had expected. To her horror, water began to seep inside the car. But she was making good progress, it seemed. Only a few yards to go, she assured herself, when suddenly the engine coughed and died. Oh, heavens, what could she do now? She was well and truly stuck and the water was lapping all around the little car. She heard a shout from the bank.

'Sit tight, Emma, I'm coming!'

Jared was there, stripped to his trunks, and as she watched he plunged into the torrent that seemed to be getting rougher by the minute. Emma could feel that the car had been washed up against the curb of the causeway.

Only a foot or two of concrete was keeping it from being borne away into the river.

She wanted to shout, 'Don't do it!' to Jared, but her voice was lost in the pounding sound of the wind and water. And then he was beside her, his head bobbing up near the car like a wet seal's.

'Did you take the fan belt off?' he shouted. 'Have another go at starting her.' She had not thought of it. The engine spluttered and then started running. 'Keep it in low gear and rev the engine to keep it dry,' he shouted, and then he was pushing the car from the back and gradually she felt it begin to move. With jerks and starts they made a laborious way to the bank, where they were joined by a couple of Africans who pushed it up the steep approach.

Emma sat there shivering in her thin dress that was damp now while Jared went back to the truck to fetch his spray for drying the engine. He lifted the bonnet and carefully wiped the points dry before using the spray. He had not said a word to her since they had reached the road and she was trembling with the reaction from the frightening experience. She looked at him, brown and spare, still clad only in short briefs, the black hair matted upon his chest and his whole body dripping.

'Aren't you cold?' she asked. 'I have a towel somewhere if it hasn't got wet.'

'No time to fuss,' he said briefly. 'This storm's going to get worse. I must see to the engine. You can dry me if you will.'

She got out of the car. It had stopped raining for the time being but still the thunder rolled around the hills and the lightning flashed with terrifying frequency. She rubbed his back with her towel while he continued to work on the engine. His skin was cold to her touch.

'That feels wonderful,' he said. 'You look a bit cold yourself. Why on earth did Terry let you drive home?'

'I wanted to come,' she told him. 'I was afraid something might be wrong at Sunglow.'

'I phoned to tell Terry you should stay there and I would call for you later, but you'd gone already. Perhaps it's just as well you got across when you did. Listen!' He lifted his head and Emma saw the intent expression of his dark features. 'The river's coming down. There must have been a storm higher up in the mountains.'

They were fortunately on high ground, otherwise Emma could imagine only too well what might have happened. It was incredible. From up river, a great wall of water arrived carrying all before it. The causeway disappeared and from their vantage point they could see huge logs swirling in the fast eddies as the water crashed down seeming as if at any moment it would burst the banks of the river.

If I'd arrived a while later, I might have gone too, thought Emma, and not for the first time she realized intensely that this was a savage wild country in spite of its veneer of a civilized way of living.

'But how could this happen?' she asked.

'Easily. A flash flood higher up the valley, more rain in the mountains, the streams that feed this river swollen with the extra water – it happens time and again in this district. One day you have the rivers practically dry and the next they're full to overflowing, taking tons of our precious topsoil down to the sea.'

'Will the crop come to any harm?'

'We'll hope not. Hail is a bigger menace than rain, and I hardly think we're going to get that now. I'll come with you. Enoch can drive the truck home.'

She put the towel on the seat and Jared got in beside her. The damp fragrance of his body was like the new-mown grass she had smelled this morning. She shivered a little, and he was quick to notice it.

'Do you want me to drive?' he asked.

'No, it doesn't matter. I'm all right now. It was a bit shattering seeing the river coming down like that. I've never seen anything happen so quickly. It was quite devastating.'

'Yes, and it must have been ruinous to the lands higher up the river. It's probably washed away some of our lucerne that we use for cattle feed. But the water goes down quickly and with luck it will leave some of the alluvial soil in the bend of our river.'

'Had you come back from Heron's Creek when the storm came up?' asked Emma.

'Yes, I came as soon as I saw those clouds arriving. Didn't even have time for a glass of champagne.'

'You don't mean that you didn't have any lunch?'

'No, I didn't, but it doesn't matter.'

'But ... but why didn't you? What have you been doing? You went out so early.'

Emma was bewildered. But possibly the Mitchells had decided to have lunch late. Perhaps they had had a festive breakfast.

'Did you have a champagne breakfast, then?'

It was the kind of exotic gesture that Yolande would have liked to make, she thought. But he had said he had had no time for champagne. Strange.

He smiled amiably as if he enjoyed puzzling her and put his hand on her knee. She went on driving trying, not to seem aware of this and yet very conscious of Jared and his damp, almost naked body just a few inches away.

'No, no breakfast either. I've been busy all day.'

Could it be that he and Yolande had driven up into the forest by themselves? As she had visualized herself and Jared doing so this morning? She knew Yolande did not worry much about food and they might have intended to eat when they came back.

'I've been right up in to the bush on the mountain at Heron's Creek,' he said as if reading her thoughts.

'Haven't been there since I was quite young. It was very interesting.'

'Was Yolande with you?' she asked.

He smiled. Emma glanced quickly away from her driving and the car swerved a little.

'Careful,' he warned. 'We don't want to land into a culvert when we've survived the river.'

His smile was wicked and exasperating, and anger twisted inside her like the flashing lightning in the dark sky overhead. How dared he make love to herself so casually last night and then go straight to Yolande and spend the day with her alone in the bush?

'Shall I drive?' he asked as the car slid across the road.

'No. I can manage quite well if you don't distract me – and please, Jared, take your hand away from my knee.'

'Oh, sorry, I was a bit absentminded.'

'Do you mean you thought I was Yolande?'

'Something like that. But your knee is much nicer. It curves rather sweetly, in fact.'

He stroked it to emphasize the statement and then took his hand away.

'Sweet, lovely Emma, smile at me,' he implored. 'I'm damp and cold and I'm probably going to catch pneumonia, and I'm damn hungry too – and you don't even appreciate that I'm all of this because I came to your rescue.'

'I do appreciate it,' Emma said quietly. 'I've never seen anything as terrifying as that raging river. But I'm not going to join your uncritical admirers, if that's what you expect. I've told you before that I'm the exception that proves the rule. I can't be charmed as easily as other women.'

'And that's a damn dangerous statement to make, Emma, if I might say so. It sort of puts a man on his mettle. And by the way, how is Terry doing? Did our large friend manage to charm you today?'

'Whether he did or not is my own affair,' she snapped, 'and I find this habit of calling him my large friend quite infuriating! Terry's a thoroughly nice man. I could go further and fare worse.'

'So that's the way the wind blows, is it? I'd better look around. I may find myself out of a job, sooner than likely. Could Terry manage two farms, do you think?'

'I'll be able to manage my own farm soon, Jared. I'm not ungrateful to you, but I'm looking forward to the time when I can do it myself.'

Deep in her heart, Emma did not know whether she was telling the truth. She only knew that she was exhausted and disturbed by all the events of the day, and that she wanted to make it clear to Jared that whatever he did would not affect her. But she could see no alternative to offering him another meal tonight. She could not expect him to prepare his own in the bleak museum room after he had come so promptly and efficiently to her rescue.

'What we both need first is a hot bath and a change of clothes,' he said. 'When I've finished, I'll light a fire in the living-room and see to the drinks. I have something to tell you, but it can wait until after supper.'

She lay in the deep hot bath and wondered what he had to say. Could he have proposed to Yolande? Oh, then, if that was so, he had been wickedly casual in his behaviour towards herself last night. Tonight she must be on her guard against him. But if he had proposed to Yolande and was going to marry her, surely that should mean an end to his flirtatious behaviour with other women? Maybe it had all happened suddenly up there in the forest where this morning she had imagined she might go with Jared. How foolish she had been!

She dressed casually in her jeans and a blue and white striped shirt open at the neck. She felt it was no use trying to look festive at this late hour. Christmas in Africa one way and another had proved rather unnerving. She brushed out her shining hair and tied it behind her head with a navy ribbon bow.

It was cold and damp this evening, although the rain had abated, misty clouds were still sweeping across the distant mountains and she was glad that Jared had suggested lighting the fire of logs that stood permanently ready in the hearth. He had placed the small tree to the side where it glittered cheerfully, and he was standing near the drinks cabinet pouring whisky into the heavy crystal goblets that had been her uncle's.

'Come and have this before you do anything about supper,' he said. 'You need it. It will do you good.'

'You must be ravenous,' she said.

'Not particularly. I'm used to going without food for long periods on hunting trips.'

Was this a hunting trip? she thought. But the quarry must have been Yolande. And it seemed it had been successful.

'Will soup and omelette be all right?' she asked. 'But if you're hungry, there is all that cold meat or I could open some tins.'

'No, the soup and omelette sounds fine. I'll make a salad and some garlic bread.'

'Oh, do you think . . .'

'We should eat garlic? Well, if both of us do, Emma, that should counteract the effect.'

She felt herself flushing. She had thought he might be going back to Yolande this evening after supper, but evidently that was not the plan.

'I meant it would not be very romantic if you went back to Yolande this evening smelling of garlic,' she blurted out.

'Who said anything about going back to Yolande? I know where I can be more comfortable. In front of the fire on Christmas night with a lovely redhead. In fact, my dear Emma, I don't intend to move from this house tonight, even to go back to my room across the yard. I've made up my mind to stay the night with you. But more of that later.'

He was standing at the fireside, his spare figure and dark face illuminated by the light of the leaping flames. But she could not read his expression. Was he joking or did he really mean it? Deep down in her body there was a trembling thrill, half terror, half rapture. She took the heavy glass in her hand and drank it quickly because she wanted to still the weak shuddering sensation of panic.

'I would like a cigarette,' she said.

'I didn't know you smoked, Emma,' he commented.

'I don't usually. I think there are some in the alabaster box over there. I got them for visitors.'

He crossed over with the box in his hand. But this was worse. Her hand trembled so much that he had to hold it steady while she lit the cigarette.

'What is it, Emma? Are you still feeling the effects of the storm?'

Yes, yes, she thought, but the storm is here in my heart. How can you be so casual when you've just announced that you mean to stay the night here? But she did not say it aloud.

'I . . . I must go to put the soup on to heat,' she said, rising from the couch. She was nearly at the door when she felt his arms around her waist, detaining her.

'Don't be so nervous, Emma my sweet, you can't come to any harm with me.'

She felt his kiss on the nape of her neck and his hands released her. In the kitchen, warming soup, breaking eggs into a blue and white bowl, heating up the heavy iron pan upon the small electric plate that did duty in the kitchen when the wood stove was unlit, she pondered that if he was intending to announce his engagement to Yolande this was a very strange way of doing it. Or perhaps it was just his nature to make the most of any opportunity. And here was the ideal chance to be rid of him altogether if she wanted to. Surely his behaviour over the last few days could be considered unsuitable for the manager of her farm?

Yet something inside her twisted away in confusion from the idea of explaining about it to Mr. Johnson. How could she accuse Jared of luring her into difficult situations when she herself felt this fatal stirring of the senses whenever she was with him? Had he meant it when he said he intended to stay the night, or had he only wanted to see her reaction, like a small boy who impales a butterfly and watches it fluttering, totally unable to get away?

She was spared further thought along these lines when he came striding into the kitchen and demanded the bread, butter, garlic and the ingredients for a salad.

'You do require a great deal of waiting on. I might just as well have done it myself,' Emma complained, as she tried to fulfil his exacting requirements while at the same time keeping her eye on the soup so that it did not boil over and frying the mushrooms for the omelette filling.

'Ah, but it wouldn't have been done half as well. Maybe in another life I was a famous chef. I should think it's almost as satisfactory as being a surgeon, for you're not expected to do any of the menial chores, just give other people orders while you accomplish wonders of culinary art or surgery.'

'And then leave other people to clean up,' said Emma, watching him using all the available sharp knives and cutting boards.

'Exactly, Emma,' said Jared, dripping oil and vinegar on to the salad with a great flourish.

At last the meal was safely in the warming trolley and they wheeled it in beside the fire.

'Sit on the rug with your back against the settee, Emma,' Jared commanded. 'I'll serve you now, since you were so critical of my accomplishments in the kitchen and implied that I gave you all the work to do.'

She sat down upon the lambswool rug and he quickly served out the omelette and salad and put the small tray upon her lap. Then he brought her a glass of red wine and kneeled down to give it to her. She looked up at him, aware that she could not move from her position because of the tray.

'Take the glass in both hands, my Emma, there.'

And taking her face in his hands he kissed her on the lips. She could not move, only let the warm sweet thrill of it sweep away caution.

'That's the chef's hors d'oeuvres,' he said when he released her.

'You're incorrigible!' Emma protested.

'Don't start an argument before you eat your omelette, Emma, it might spoil and it looks almost as good as my salad.'

Eating the simple meal and looking into the glowing logs that were redolent of applewood, Emma felt her nervousness subside. It seemed very strange that often she so disliked Jared, and yet sometimes, as now, for instance, she felt warm sweet simple happiness just because he was there. But that was the danger, she reflected. That was when she was off her guard and he had a sixth sense to know when she was at her most vulnerable.

'I'll go and make the coffee,' she said, wanting to get away from the atmosphere of warmth and sensuous comfort.

'Too late. When I give my mind to it, I'm the soul of efficiency. The coffee is perking on the hot spot of the warming tray. Now all I need for my comfort is Emma beside me and a dram of Courvoisier.'

'Heavens, I quite forgot!' she exclaimed. 'Jared, your Christmas gift is over there near the tree. I haven't had a chance to give it to you today.'

He opened the parcels and at once declared they must sample the old brandy, but Emma cautiously refused. She felt she could not trust herself again to breathe in those warm glowing exhalations. She sat relaxed with a cup of coffee, felt him settle himself beside her, his shoulder against hers, his eyes studying the golden liquid in the large goblet.

'What a happy choice, Emma! I hope you'll like mine just as well.'

From his pocket he produced a small box, professionally wrapped in decorative Christmas paper and a rosette of red ribbon.

'Oh, Jared, there was no need . . .' she began.

'Don't talk. Open it!'

Inside was an exquisite small perfectly carved rhino in green verdite.

'A present from Africa,' said Jared, his eyes on her face, examining her expression of delight. 'The oldest known rock in the world, found only in one place.'

'It's beautiful,' Emma said, stroking it gently. 'Like dark jade.'

'If any stroking is to be done, try the donor,' said Jared. 'I'm glad you like it. Do you recall, Emma, when we first met, I asked you what my reward would be if I accepted your invitation to the dance and you said, oh, so sweetly and tentatively, "A kiss"?'

'I didn't think you would remember that,' she said quietly. 'It's so long ago.'

'I remember more than you think. Do I get the same reward now, do you think?'

She looked at him, hesitating. Oh, no, she must not start all that heartbreak over again. He was playing with her as cunningly as she knew he could play a silver fish glittering on the end of his line. She was totally aware of him with the leaping firelight on his dark brooding face that could be so serious, almost menacing, at one moment and then the next alight with charm that was so hard to resist. She looked at the rhino in her hand, so smooth and polished to the touch, and remembered how, all those years ago, she had been surprised when she had touched his rough chin with her lips, the very first time she had encountered that individual hard male kiss.

'You think too much, Emma. You should learn to let go more. What's a kiss between friends?'

'If it means so little to you, I wonder that you want it.'

'I want it all right. The question is, do you? I've told you before I don't do anything that's against your will, but, my God, Emma, you can still try a man to the limit, and you should know better now. There you sit looking beautiful, your hair like those flames in front of us and your eyes huge and dark and utterly appealing. Those eyes ... if you stood naked in front of me, I should look at all the loveliness of your body, but still return to gazing at those eyes.'

'That will never happen, Jared,' Emma said in a low voice.

'I'm sorry, Emma, I didn't mean to scare you, especially tonight. I'm afraid I forget that you're still very young. I guess I can do without that kiss. I don't deserve it, do I?'

Emma thought of the journey home and of the river pouring between its banks in turbulent fury and of Jared's brown body swimming through the strong waves to bring her help. Where would she be now if it had not been for him? She leaned towards him and put her hand on his face.

'You do deserve it, Jared, you do.'

His lips were hard and closed to her touch and it was she who smoothed her mouth against his until he responded with increasing fervour. There was no going back now, she thought wildly. Her pulsating body told her so. Come what may, she was committed to his kindled passion. She must put her trust in him, for she could no longer trust herself.

As they kissed with increasing ardour and his hands sought the firm sweet curves of her body, she was suddenly aware of a sound outside their own breathless whispers of desire.

Someone was knocking on the door, hammering with desperate urgency.

'Oh, God in heaven!' groaned Jared. 'I half expected this. It sounds like trouble.'

CHAPTER EIGHT

HER racing pulses slowed as she sat where Jared had left her until a log fell apart with a shower of sparks and she roused herself to move and rearrange the fire. She could hear voices and thought that she could recognize the deep-toned note of the African foreman. Certainly Jared was speaking in Xhosa to somebody, asking rapid questions. In a few moments he strode back into the room.

'I'll have to go, Emma. I intended to tell you this evening, but I hesitated to alarm you. What Terry said was true – there is a stray leopard in the district. They called me out this morning because it killed a calf at Heron's Creek. I've been trying to arrange about tranquillizing guns and darts. We don't want to kill it unless it becomes absolutely necessary. I decided to dart it and move it to a game reserve.'

'But where is it now?' she asked.

'That's the trouble. Enoch says it's been seen in this vicinity and we're afraid it may go for the Brahmins. I've been tracking it up in the bush all day so that we could get an idea of where it hides out, but it must have doubled back on its tracks and crossed the river before the storm and now it won't be able to get back until the river has gone down, so Enoch and I will have to sit up on guard. If it comes near we'll hope to scare it away with brands and banging and shouting.'

'Oh, Jared, won't that be awfully dangerous?'

'Someone must do it. Apart from the humanitarian reasons, do you realize, Emma, how much those Brahmins are worth? And that particular stock is virtually irreplaceable.'

She wanted to say that they were not worth his life, but

she could see it was impossible to change his decision.

'Will you take a gun?' she asked.

'Of course – I'm not that crazy. But I hope not to have to use it. Emma, my sweet one, go to bed and don't worry. One way and another we've had quite a day, haven't we? Do I get a kiss to send me on my way?'

She clung to him, kissing him with renewed fervour. He laughed and, putting her face against his chest, stroked her hair.

'Take care of yourself, Jared,' she whispered.

His hand traced the curve of her cheek and found it wet.

'What's all this? I can see I must chase leopards more often. Now be a good girl and get off to bed. I'll report back tomorrow morning. But lock your door and don't go out of the house. You never know where a rogue animal like this one may turn up. I'm going to shut the dogs in the shed outside – it's too dangerous to take them with me. I was going to sleep downstairs here in case of trouble, but, now we know for certain the animal is around, I must go to the kraal.'

When he had gone, she felt the coffee pot and finding it still hot, poured herself a cup. If it kept her awake it could not be helped. She did not expect to be able to sleep, anyway. Every nerve in her body seemed stretched taut as the strings of a violin.

One question was solved. He had had every intention of staying the night, but not for the reason she had suspected. If he had explained to her about the leopard when he first came, what a lot of emotional upheaval she would have been saved. But would she? Now that she felt calmer, she wondered what on earth had possessed her to show him so clearly the extent to which his physical self attracted her. She had been so near the brink of surrender to those feelings. But now she could see that her resolve had been weakened by the happenings of the day, especially the fact that Jared had saved her from the flooding river.

And all the time that she had imagined him in the forest with Yolande, he had been tracking the leopard. If only she had known this! But what difference did it make, really? Whatever he had done today, whatever had happened, it did not alter the fact that everyone thought he would probably marry Yolande, and that she, Emma, felt he was just making use of his opportunities when he so casually made love to her.

Apart from endearments, which on his lips meant nothing, had he ever uttered one word of affection to her? No, it seemed to her that he had always made it clear that he regarded women as a pleasant hobby. This evening she had been led away by the intimacy of the scene and most of all by the fact that she had felt grateful to him, so grateful that she had kissed him, encouraged him to make love to her against her usual better judgment. For a while the feelings he aroused had almost overwhelmed her, but now she had been given a chance to draw back, she must never let such a thing happen again.

The fire was burning low now and her coffee was finished. She took the little green verdite rhino in her hand. It was like those Japanese carvings, she thought – what were they called? Netsuke, that was it. In the East, people carried them in their pockets and held them for comfort. It was supposed to make them feel tranquil, just as the Greeks used 'worry beads'. She held the small rhino that felt warm to her touch and hoped that feeling the polished stone would calm her in the same way. But then she thought of Jared, lying wakeful, guarding the sleek cream-coloured cattle, and she thought of the leopard hiding somewhere in her lands, wild and savagely beautiful and needing to find food, and a tremor of fear shook her.

The room that had seemed so luxuriously warm and

comfortable while Jared was with her now looked deserted and bleak with the fire falling into ashes and the remains of the supper around her. She put the debris on to the trolley and wheeled it into the kitchen, taking her time about scraping off the plates and washing the glasses so that there would not be so much for Rosie to do in the morning before she went off for the day.

At last she had finished all the tidying up and went reluctantly upstairs. She undressed and went to the window, but when she opened it the wind was bitterly cold and she shivered in her thin negligée. She remembered that in the room that had been Jared's, she had seen a warm gown hanging on a hook on the door, so she went in to get it and wrapped herself in that. It was a man's gown of a pure light wool in a ruby red with a paisley pattern, and it reached to her ankles. She rolled up the sleeves and tied the sash securely around her small waist, then returned to the window. However cold it was she must listen and try to hear if there were any strange sounds that would give her a clue about what was happening to Jared. The gown wrapped her in its warmth and had a masculine scent of tobacco and sandalwood. How could the smell of a garment serve as such a passionate reminder of its owner?

She opened the window wider and leaned out listening to the sounds of the night. A full moon had risen spreading an eerie light over the countryside. It was odd to think that this morning she had been bathing in the pool, hardly even able to stand the heat of the sun, and now the moon was shining so coldly upon the roofs that they almost looked as if they were frosted. Of course this was an illusion, but all the same the temperature had dropped amazingly quickly. This was how it was in Africa, a country of heat and sudden storms that could be followed by a night that was piercingly cold. She listened carefully, but could not hear anything but the distant howl of a dog and the cry of a barn owl. They were such lonely sounds heard in this cold silvery light.

'Jared would say I was foolish,' she thought. 'I'm doing no good here. I'd better get to bed.'

She took an extra blanket and filled a hot water bottle from the tap, and gradually she became warm. Why was she worrying about Jared? He had been on countless hunting expeditions and knew the habits of wild animals. Telling herself this and trying to believe she could trust him not to be reckless, at last she fell asleep.

In spite of her worry and probably because she was exhausted after her long day, she slept for some hours and only woke when the furniture in the room was beginning to grow distinct in the first grey light of morning. Something had roused her, for she still felt heavy with sleep. Down below from the shed across the yard, the dogs were making a terrible noise, howling, barking, scratching at the door and hurling their heavy bodies against it. They were two hunting dogs, half mastiff, half ridgeback, and they were used to being left to roam free at night, but Jared had shut them in so that they would not follow him.

The din was ghastly, like the howling of a hundred banshees. Emma, her nerves already stretched to breaking point, felt she could not stand this noise a moment longer. Jared had said she must not go outside, but he had meant during the night. Now that it was almost light, the danger, if there had ever been any, must surely be past. She wrapped the warm dressing-gown around her and putting on a pair of strong sandals, went down the stairs and unlocked the door. She looked around the yard and saw one of the tabby cats that usually lived in the stables. It must have strayed over here and been mewing to be let in, and the dogs had probably heard it and started this hullabaloo. She must go to quieten them. They were usually very well behaved because they had been trained to obey and she was not at all perturbed at the idea of having to deal with them.

She shooed the cat inside the kitchen and started to walk across the yard towards the room. The door was not locked and she opened it cautiously, sliding her body through the narrow aperture she had made and at the same time speaking firmly to the dogs. They quietened as soon as they saw her and pushed themselves against her, their thrashing tails almost knocking her off her feet. They had overturned the water in their excitement and she refilled the bowl, wondering whether she could let them go free, but on second thoughts she had better wait until Jared arrived back, since they might follow his scent and join him. She felt almost sure now that little had happened during the night and that the leopard had probably spent the night in some hideout in the bushy hills around the neighbourhood. She would surely have heard some commotion if it had been around the cattle kraal.

The dogs seemed calmer now she had spoken to them and soothed them. As she had surmised, they had probably been disturbed by the little cat. She wondered whether she could go back to bed. Surely Jared must be coming back soon?

'Be good now,' she told the dogs. 'Your master will be here right now.'

As she went to the door to go out she noticed that one of the hinges had broken under their onslaught. The building was old and she supposed the hasps had been weakened by rust. They would have to have it fixed, buy new ones next time they were in town. She would look at the fittings on the small window too while she was here and see if they were in a like state. She went across to it and started to examine the catch. The dogs, who had been quiet enough for some minutes now, started barking again, a note of absolute frenzy in their yelps. She turned on them, annoyed, thinking that they had recommenced their fuss because she had stopped soothing them. But as she turned she happened to glance out of the window. For the moment she could not believe what she was seeing. A full-grown leopard was loping across the yard.

As she stood frozen by this incredible sight, it stopped in its tracks and lifted its head as if some scent had come to its nostrils, then turned and, looking almost like some huge cat after a mouse, slid its limbs into a crouched predatory position and moved in this manner towards the place where she and the dogs were sheltering. What was to happen? She knew with a dreadful tremor at the heart that only a weakened door stood between her and this sleek cruel animal, and that the dogs had got the scent already and would hurl themselves against that door in a moment, making it even less strong.

She called to them, but this time they did not respond to her call and she had to drag them back from the door with all her strength, holding on to their collars with the utmost difficulty. As she soothed and managed to quieten them for a few seconds, she heard the soft pad of the leopard's movements as it leaped on to the wooden steps that led on to the small verandah that ran beside this room and the museum room. Emma had bolted the window, but she dared not look outside. If the leopard saw her or scented her there, it might leap up and possibly break the fastening. She saw a shadow moving along the slight gap at the bottom of the door and heard a sniffing sound and a terrifying noise, half growl, half cough. The dogs went wild again and she could not hold them. They barked frantically, hurling themselves against the door, while the hinges creaked each time this happened.

She had never been more terrified in her life. She was frozen with fear, not able to think clearly any more how to act. She knew it was hopeless, but she must have screamed and shouted, 'Jared, oh, Jared, for God's sake, come, come quickly!' And then miraculously above the din she heard his voice, strong and clear, 'It's all right, Emma. I'm here.' And above the noise of the dogs and the growling cough of the leopard, there was the sharp crack of a rifle and then another and another.

'Stay there, Emma. Don't come out!'

It seemed to her that Jared's voice had never sounded more welcome, but what was happening out there? She could hear Jared's voice like the crack of a whip, another shot and a wild snarl that seemed to freeze the blood in her veins. This was followed by a silence that was just as frightening to Emma, crouched on the floor of the shed, her wrists feeling almost torn apart from her efforts to control the dogs. She could not look through the window, for if she did the dogs would get away and she knew she must not let this happen.

After what seemed hours, the door burst open, the dogs slipped from her grasp and hurled themselves on Jared, but he quickly shut the door so that they could not escape. He stood swaying on his feet, unshaven with the pungent smell of gunpowder all around him. She rushed at him, crying, 'Jared, are you hurt?' but he pushed her roughly away.

'Not now, Emma, for God's sake! No, I'm not hurt, but it's no thanks to you. What the hell do you think you're doing here? Didn't I tell you to stay in the house and not move from there until I came back?'

She was taken aback by his anger.

'I ... I ... the dogs were making a noise,' she stammered.

'Of course they were making a noise! Any dog would if it smelled a leopard. What the blazes did you think you could do about it if you came here?'

'I thought they were barking at a cat. Of course I had no idea the leopard was around. Oh, Jared!'

She was suddenly overwhelmed by the thought that

she had crossed the yard by herself while all the time the animal might have been watching her from the bushes nearby. Tears rolled down her cheeks and she began to tremble.

'No tears, please, Emma. I've had just about as much as I can take. Of all the boneheaded ways of behaving yours takes the ruddy biscuit! You thought a cat was in the yard . . . some cat!'

'What's happened to the leopard?' asked Emma, trying to keep the tremble out of her voice.

'I scared it away with the shots over its head – I should think it's quite a good way from here by now, God knows where. I suppose we'll find out soon enough when it kills another calf.'

'I thought you'd killed it,' she whispered.

Or it had killed you, she thought. She would never forget that dreadful silence that had seemed to last for hours.

'No, I'm only going to do that as a last resort. Leopards are a dying species – too many stupid women want their pelts. I hope you aren't one of those kind, Emma.'

Emma, recovered now from her extreme alarm, suddenly felt her temper rising to flash point.

'Do I look the kind of woman who wants to drape herself in leopardskin? Really, Jared, you haven't the slightest idea of what I'm really like, if you can say a thing like that!'

Jared sighed wearily and rubbed a streak of gunpowder across his brow.

'Maybe not. Just at this time I can't feel that it matters overmuch. I've had quite a night, Emma, and if you want to be ill-tempered you'd better choose some other time.'

'Ill-tempered? Me? It's you that have never stopped criticizing me since you opened that door! You're quite impossible sometimes, Jared – not even sometimes, practically all the time,' she added.

'And the other times?'

His expression together with the dark streaks on his face and his unshaven appearance made him look like the lowest of ruffians.

'There seems only one way in which I can make myself popular with you. Emma, in spite of your virtuous denials of it.'

He came towards her and, before she realized his intentions, he had picked her up and was carrying her along the small length of the wooden verandah to his own room. Released from their prison, the dogs ran out into the yard and the deep bell notes of their barking seemed to mingle with the frightened thudding of her heart. The door gave under the thrusts of his shoulder and he strode across and flung her on to the bed, then lay beside her, pinioning her arms, the rough strength of his hands bruising her tender skin.

She had been terrified of the leopard, but it was nothing to the terror she felt now as his mouth came down on hers and she felt the steel-like hardness of his body and saw the golden animal glow of his eyes so close to her own.

'You've been trying to find a way to get rid of me since the day you came here,' he muttered. 'You've been deliberately leading me on and retreating on every occasion you could find. Well, now I've damn well had enough of it! You can run to Mr. Johnson this very day. Wake him up if you have to, and tell him I've forced myself upon you. I've never known any woman so utterly maddening and provocative as you, Emma, and I intend to make love to you, whether you like it or not. In spite of your denials, you've shown me pretty plainly that you're not averse to passion and are not inexperienced, so why should I continue to deny myself?'

The shock of his wild behaviour following so closely on the frightful minutes she had endured beforehand shattered Emma entirely and she broke into wild sobs. Almost at once he released her and got up from the bed.

'You're very clever, Emma, about knowing what to do on any occasion. I have no armour against tears. Go now. I don't want any more to do with you for a long time, maybe not ever. I've simply had enough. When we're calmer we'll discuss what's to be done. Obviously you'll use this opportunity to dispense with me.'

CHAPTER NINE

SHE had gone back to the house, terrified to cross the yard where she had seen the leopard such a short time before, and yet even more terrified to stay in the company of this man who had acted like a wild stranger. She had a hot bath and lay on her bed, but she could not stop trembling. Counting the yellow roses on the wallpaper, she tried to dull the memory of the scene with Jared. He despises me, she thought. He's attracted to me physically, but he despises me. All along I've shown him far too plainly that he attracts me – and of course to a man like Jared that was practically an open invitation. Because he feels I respond to him, he believes I'm wanton. But what am I to do? He's evidently willing to go now – it was only for the sake of his promise to Uncle Mac that he stayed here. I thought it was I who wanted to get rid of him, but now it seems it's mutual. Over and over she heard his voice, 'I don't want any more to do with you for a long time, maybe not ever.' At last, from sheer exhaustion, Emma slept, and was only awakened some hours later by Rosie knocking on the bedroom door.

She was carrying a tray and the sun winked on the bright fruit juice, the brown toast in its silver holder and the yellow scrambled eggs.

'Morning, Miss Emma. I thought you must have had plenty good Christmas Day, because you were sleeping so nicely.'

On the tray beside the small silver coffee pot, there was a perfect apricot-coloured rose, and Emma's heart skipped a beat as she saw an envelope beside it. Only one person wrote in that thick definite hand. She could recognize it even though all it said was 'Emma', and she opened the note hastily. There were two words in the middle of the thick sheet of paper. 'Forgive me'. That was all. She felt as if a great weight had been lifted from her heart. If Jared asked this of her, he could not hate her as much as she had thought a few hours ago. She must see him as soon as possible, for she felt she could not stand not knowing how he felt about her, whether he really did despise her, whether she really did stand condemned in his eyes because she had behaved foolishly.

Today was still a holiday according to the calendar and the workers would take things easy. Emma wondered if Jared had gone to the lands or if he was sleeping after his exhausting day and night. She felt she must see him and somehow make things right between them, although when she thought of it there had been so many misunderstandings that she wondered whether she could ever do this.

'Have you seen Mr. Jared this morning?' she asked Rosie.

'He had a cup of coffee and some rusks very early, then he put this flower on your tray and gave me the note to give to you and he told me to tell you he has gone and does not know how long he will be away.'

Emma felt as if a glass of cold water had been splashed all over her.

'But where has he gone?' she faltered.

'To Heron's Creek – I expect to see that Miss Yolande. Miss Emma, if you don't have him, I am telling you she will,' said Rosie firmly.

There's nothing I can do about it, thought Emma. Why had Jared sent her the note if he intended to run back to Yolande at the first opportunity? Her temporary elation at receiving his plea for forgiveness disappeared. Any man would feel he had to apologize after their scene last night. But Jared is not any man, she thought. When I'm with him, it's as if I'm on a roundabout. I'm whirled around, I ride up, then down, and I can't decide from one moment to the next what I really feel about him. Heaven knows after yesterday I should want him to go, but do I? Oh, why did he have to go before I had had a chance to discuss things? I know – I'll phone him at Heron's Creek.

When she had dressed, she came downstairs still re-solved to do this. But she hovered around the phone regarding it as if it were some black two-headed snake. Finally she plucked up courage and dialled the number. It was Yolande who replied.

'Oh, Emma – no, he's not here. I'm hopping mad that this beastly animal has ruined the holiday. Didn't you know they've all gone up into the bush after it? The darts and drugs came late yesterday, and Jared, Dad and some others have gone up to try to get it. I think your Terry is one of them. I'm bored stiff here on my own. Are you alone? What do you say to our driving up to see how things are going? I have a Land-Rover here and I know how to drive it.'

Emma reflected that this was probably the very last thing that Jared would want them to do. But when she thought of the long day ahead, she felt she would go mad if she were to remain inactive not knowing anything about what was happening as the men trailed the leopard into the bush. She made up her mind that whether it was approved of or not she would go with Yolande. As she drove over to Heron's Creek, she realized that it was the first time she had been here since that fateful afternoon five years ago. But there was no time for sentiment. She only gave a fleeting thought to the young girl who had suffered so much heartbreak here. Now she was mature and she should have more sense – but had she?

Emma had put on her denim slacks suit, as she thought this would be the best and toughest thing to wear if she had to go into rough country, and Yolande was in a greenish khaki safari suit that, with her silver-blonde hair, made her look more feminine than ever. This year there had been a craze for army colours and military fashions and Yolande liked to be first with the new styles.

'Cooee, Emma, am I glad to see you! I don't think they can have found this wretched animal yet. I've been watching the hill with my binoculars and I can still see the truck going along the track. We should be able to catch up with them.'

'They aren't going to like it if we join them,' said Emma a bit doubtfully.

'Oh, to hell with them,' said Yolande cheerfully. 'Why should they get all the excitement? This isn't the middle ages, though sometimes in this country you would think it was. Come on, I've loaded a case of beer and some sandwiches. That can be our excuse for going there. Come inside and have a cup of coffee before we start.'

The large room with its old rafters and stone fireplace looked just the same as it had done on that far-off afternoon when Emma had shown Jared how deeply she cared. Even the sofa in front of the fireplace, deep and comfortable, seemed to have the same cover. What fatal chance had linked her life with a man like Jared? She had been doomed to emotional entanglement with him since she had impetuously issued that invitation to the dance. If only she had not met him again! But it was not too late. She would take him at his word and ask him to go away from the farm, and she would devote herself to running the place on her own. If she need not meet him again, she could get over the twisted puzzling sensations that plagued her every time he was near.

'It's a nice place, isn't it?' said Yolande, who had observed Emma looking around the room. 'Of course, if I were to take over I'd want something a bit more modern, but you could easily fix this room up. That corner would take the hi-fi and you could have a semi-circular settee in this bay with a telly, and I'd have wall-to-wall carpeting instead of these handwoven rugs and get rid of all these junky old pictures.'

'But, Yolande, I think this room is lovely,' protested Emma.

'Dinkum? Well, I guess it's spacious and those old beams are impressive, but Jared has been a bachelor for too long. A man is inclined to hate things changed.'

'But these rugs have such beautiful soft colours, and you couldn't cover these beautiful yellow-wood floors, could you?'

'Try me! I like something your feet sink into.'

Emma said with an effort, 'If you ... if you were to marry Jared, would you stay here?'

Yolande shrugged her shoulders.

'Search me. On the whole I think I would prefer it here. It's a softer life for a woman than it is in Australia, plenty of domestics and help with the children. But just lately Jared has spoken as if he wouldn't mind having a go at living down under again. So I don't know what would happen if we decided to marry. I'm going to be twenty-one in a while and then I come into my mother's money, so I guess I'll have more to play around with. I'm going to have one hell of a party. You must come, Emma, of course.'

'Thank you,' said Emma.

'Don't say anything to Jared, will you?' Yolande went on. 'Nothing's fixed yet. I don't want to jump the gun before he's asked me, but here's hoping!'

She finished her coffee and swung confidently out to the Land-Rover. Emma followed. She would have loved to ask more questions, but did not want to appear too curious. Did Jared and Yolande intend to announce their engagement on this twenty-first birthday? She thought it probable. But then every time she had spoken about Yolande to Jared he seemed to have played it down. However, maybe he did not want to appear to be attached to another woman when he was constantly trying to attract her, Emma. Oh, how confusing it was! She wished she could be finished with the whole sorry business.

They drove out of the farmlands and up the rough track that led in the direction where Yolande had seen the truck. The men had taken a heavy vehicle with a wired back in which they usually transported cattle and sheep, but for this expedition it had been reinforced with strong steel bars. Yolande drove over the rough road with the utmost verve. They slammed around corners and sometimes Emma wondered whether they would reach the place in one piece, but she need not have worried, for Yolande's driving was fairly reliable if a bit daredevil.

On each side of them as they ascended up into the hills was bushy growth and tangled trees. What a countryside in which to try and find an animal! Emma thought. But at last they came to a place on the hillside where there was a flat plateau of land, grassy and clear of bush, and here they found that the truck had been parked. A group of men were sitting in its shade, talking quietly.

'Hi there!' called Yolande, bouncing out of their vehicle.

'Sh . . . sh!' they all warned.

'What gives?' she asked, not in the least abashed by this general disapproval.

'The trackers are following the way they think the leopard has gone, further up the hill. We're waiting for some signal from them,' Emma heard Jared say.

She had followed Yolande, walking slowly from the vehicle until she came to the group of men. Even then she could not bring herself to look at Jared. But she could not avoid him for long.

'Emma, what's brought you here?' he demanded.

She looked at him now and her heart turned a somer- sault as she did so. His thin whipcord body contrasted strangely with Terry's barrel physique and the rotund short figure of Yolande's father, Craig Mitchell. He looked at her for a long time and his dark expressive eyes seemed to be giving her some message that was of infinite significance. She felt that they were alone together, that all the others here had faded into the background – and yet they were here within hearing and she could not say a word. Ardently she wished she could have spoken to him alone.

'Well?' he asked, sounding impatient, and she realized that he had asked her a question. She thought she had probably imagined that dark passionate expression, or mis-read it, for here he was speaking to her just as sharply as if he had never written that note or placed an apricot rose upon her tray.

'Yolande asked me to come,' she explained. 'We brought sandwiches and beer.'

'And that was a very bright idea, I must say,' said Terry, coming up to Emma. 'I phoned you this morning, Emma, but there was no reply. But I see you must have got home safely. I just about had a cadenza when I heard the leopard was supposed to be on your side of the river.'

She turned to Terry, glad of some distraction from the almost hypnotic gaze that she wanted to avoid.

'Thanks, Terry, but I was quite safe. I'm getting used to adventure. It's an exciting life in Africa if you can take it.'

'You arrived home without any trouble?' he asked.

'Well, not exactly. I had a bit of difficulty at the river, but Jared came with a truck and helped me negotiate it.'

'Good for Jared!' He glanced across at Jared, who was now caught up in Yolande's excited conversation. 'He's not such a bad chap, is he? I was glad to think last night that he was there to protect you.'

Emma smiled. If Terry knew ... but he never would. What had happened or nearly happened last night was a secret between herself and Jared. No, she would never use it as a lever against him. If all that Yolande said had been correct, it seemed likely that he would be leaving shortly anyway. They could try to avoid each other for the rest of the time he was there on the farm. He had been very definite in saying that he wanted nothing more to do with her. But even while she was thinking about avoiding him, she longed desperately to speak to him now. It was no use, however. As usual Yolande was monopolizing him completely.

'It was damn foolish of you girls to come here,' she heard Jared say.

'Don't be like that!' smiled Yolande. 'Have some of this beautiful beer. It must be thirsty work tracking a leopard.'

Craig Mitchell came to join Terry and Emma. He had a can of beer in one hand and a flask of brandy in the other, and Emma was surprised. She had only met him once, but he had not seemed particularly a drinking man.

'Getting up a bit of Dutch courage,' he explained rather sheepishly. 'Searching for a leopard in this kind of country is sure thirsty work.'

'I'd go easy on the drink mixing, Craig,' Jared called. 'The day's young yet and we probably still have a lot of ground to cover.'

'Don't worry about me, old boy, I can take it. Aussies can hold their liquor – you should know that.'

'It's true, Jared, you needn't worry about Dad. Drink hardly ever affects him,' Yolande assured him.

'Social drinking is a bit different from mixing beer and brandy when you're tracking a dangerous animal in the full heat of the sun,' Emma heard Jared say to Yolande, but Craig did not appear to have heard him, or if he had he took no notice and continued to drink freely from his can of beer with occasional nips of brandy.

There was a low whistle from the bush and two Africans emerged into the clearing. Jared spoke to them quietly in their own language and, from their gestures and low but excited voices, Emma realized, with a sinking of the heart, that they were telling him they had found some clue to where the leopard was hiding out. Jared gathered the men together to tell them about it. Yolande remained with him, her hand on his bare arm, her blonde head almost touching his shoulder. But Emma stayed on the edge of the group, feeling that Jared thought she should not be here at all.

'The leopard is up there in the kranz,' Jared told them. 'There's a big rock and a small slit in the cliff behind it where it's hidden – at least that's what the trackers think. They haven't actually seen it, but the prints are there. And we daren't use dogs, of course. That would be absolute murder. They can't stand up to a leopard, however tough they are.'

'What do you intend to do, then?' asked Terry.

'We'll have to go up there and play it by ear. We'll try to flush the beast out somehow. I have the darting gun loaded and ready. Of course, if anyone should be in danger, we'll have to shoot properly, but I hope that won't happen.'

The men moved away to the truck to get their hats and do last-minute adjustments to the kit. Craig Mitchell called to Yolande and reluctantly she moved away from Jared. It had happened, the thing Emma had longed for. She was now alone with Jared, but all the words she had thought of were frozen on her lips. They were standing a few yards from each other, but before Emma could decide what to do, Jared had walked up to her. Glancing quickly around and seeing that the others were still occupied, he grasped hold of her shoulders. His dark head bent towards her and she could not avoid meeting the vital gaze of his expressive eyes.

'Emma, did you get my note?' he asked.

She nodded, unable to speak.

'And the answer?'

'There's not time now ... later,' she whispered, seeing the others coming towards them.

'As you wish,' he replied, his hands dropping from her shoulders. His voice was cold and he shrugged as if he would have liked to discard any connection with her, she thought.

'Good luck,' she said.

'We'll need it.' He turned to Yolande, who had seen a certain amount of the little scene with Emma and was frowning. 'You and Emma must remain here,' he directed.

'What! Are we going to miss all the excitement?'

'You're going to miss the danger, I hope,' said Jared adamantly. 'I think it might be as well if you persuaded your father to stay here too.'

'That will take some doing,' said Yolande. 'Pop's pretty damn obstinate. He's like me – he likes his own way.'

Mr. Mitchell was carrying his liquor well as he had said he would. He did not show any signs that the excessive amount of beer and brandy he had consumed had had any effect on him, and thrust aside the suggestion that he should stay behind.

'Not on your life,' he declared. 'I'm not missing my first bit of African adventure right on my own doorstep.'

Jared shrugged and gave up trying to persuade him. Yolande and Emma watched as the men disappeared into the bushy track that led up to the krantz. It looked rough going, and Emma noticed that Craig Mitchell stumbled a little before he was lost to sight. Was he really as sober as he seemed? she wondered. Yolande sat down on the steps of the truck and opened a can of beer.

'Don't you want one?' she asked Emma, but Emma declined, although her mouth felt dry with nervousness, so dry that the sandwich she tried to eat tasted like cotton wool and she had to give up the attempt.

'Jared's such a damn tyrant,' grumbled Yolande. 'But I guess it could be different once we were married. There would be ways and means of getting my own way then.'

Emma wished she would stop talking. Her whole consciousness seemed concentrated on listening for the sounds that would indicate what was going on further up the mountain, although she knew nothing could be happening yet.

'Do you think it's a good idea to marry an older man?' asked Yolande.

Emma tried to concentrate on the conversation.

'I guess it's all right to marry anyone so long as you love them enough,' she said.

Yolande tilted the beer can and poured the last drops of light golden liquid down her throat.

'Love?' she asked, laughing the infectious gurgle that was part of her attraction. 'I've never thought much about it. I just get crazy for a man, the way he looks, the way he smiles, the way he makes love.'

There was no doubt about it. Emma felt a pang of emotion almost as bad as she had five years ago when she had seen Jared with that other silver blonde. But it was humiliation she felt now, she assured herself, certainly not rejected love.

'I don't know whether I would really be capable of spending my whole life with one man,' Yolande went on. 'But Pop is so possessive and disapproving usually and, as I told you, he seems to have taken a real shine to Jared. Me too, of course. He really turns me on. He's frightfully attractive physically, don't you think so?'

'Yes, I suppose he is,' Emma admitted.

'You must have got to know him quite well since you came here,' said Yolande with a curious look. 'How have you got on with him?'

'Not always very well,' Emma shrugged. 'He's rather domineering at times.'

'I guess I can sort that out if we decide to marry,' Yolande said. 'After all, it must be a bit trying to a man like

Jared to have a woman boss, and that's what you are, isn't that so? I think the sooner he starts running his own farm again, the better.'

'That would suit me quite well now,' Emma replied.

'I'm glad you think so. It's lucky that you're so interested in Terry, otherwise I think Jared's charm would have worked on you too.'

'Listen,' said Emma. 'I thought I heard something.' She had wanted to end the conversation, but now, as Yolande's voice was still, they became aware of sounds up on the hillside, excited shouts and warning screams of baboons.

'Something's happening,' said Yolande, springing up. 'I'm going up there. Why should we miss all the fun? The men have all got guns and they're all good shots if the tranquillizer doesn't work. We won't be in any danger.'

She was running along the track now, and Emma followed. But it was not excitement she was after. It was rather that she could no longer stand the suspense of not knowing what was happening up on the mountain.

'Perhaps they just disturbed a troupe of baboons,' she panted.

'Oh, don't say that! I want to be in at the kill.'

'But nothing's going to get killed,' Emma insisted.

'You never know. If the dart doesn't work, they may have no alternative. I don't know why they're all so fussy about wanting to keep it alive. I wouldn't mind a leopard-skin handbag and hat. I guess it wouldn't be enough for a coat.'

The men were below the top of the hill where there were folded rocks and fissures that could have hidden a dozen animals.

'Where's Jared?' demanded Yolande.

'He's gone around the back of the rocks with Enoch,' Terry replied. 'They're going to try to flush it out. It's in a small cave over there.'

'Who has the darting gun?' asked Emma.

'Jared has that and no other gun, so if he gets an opportunity to use it it's to be hoped it works in time.'

'We have the other guns,' said Craig Mitchell. 'I guess we should go up there to back him up.'

'He said not,' said Terry. 'I think he thought he could do without a crowd if the leopard came out into the open.'

'Baloney,' said Craig. 'There's safety in numbers.'

He started to scramble over the rough ground, and Emma noticed that he did not seem too steady on his feet. As he was some yards above them going in the direction of the cave, there was a sudden shout from above.

'Get to cover! I've managed to dart it. Won't be long now, but it's still frisky.'

Terry, the Africans and the girls all hid behind the thick bushes, but Craig Mitchell was still weaving his way up the track.

'Dad, come here, for God's sake!' Yolande shouted frantically. There was a sound of breaking branches from the undergrowth and suddenly the magnificent animal appeared, snarling furiously, its yellow eyes half closed, but still apparently able to see Craig, who was directly in its path. It was almost upon him when it paused as if bewildered and sank to the ground.

'That was a near thing,' said Craig, and began to laugh. Emma thought he sounded hysterical, as well he might. At that moment Jared came into view. He had put down the darting gun and was quite unarmed.

'Well, we seem to have made it,' he called to the others. He was smiling triumphantly, but all at once his expression changed.

'Craig, for God's sake, what are you doing? Look out, man, it won't have taken proper effect yet!'

Craig, as if to show that his fright of a few moments ago had not really existed, was approaching the prostrate form of the leopard with a fatuous smile on his face.

'Let's have a closer look at this pretty kitty,' he said.

When he was within a few yards of it, the leopard moved. It rolled over into a crouching position with a revival of strength and growled menacingly at Craig. Craig stood frozen in his tracks, an expression of absolute terror replacing his smile. Emma never knew how Jared did it, but in a second, it seemed, he was beside the frightened man and had pushed him sprawling some yards away upon the ground. The leopard was nearer now and Emma closed her eyes, then opened them in horror as the furious animal lashed out at Jared, who had not had time to get out of the way.

She saw him wince with an expression of pain as the leopard caught him by the shoulder, tearing away his shirt in a long rip. What could save him now? thought Emma desperately. She saw Terry, who had been standing seemingly paralyzed by the swift events, raise his gun. And yet he could not use it, for Craig was still stumbling around uncertainly and Jared was too near the animal to make a shot safe. The next second the leopard had rolled over, unconscious.

'Don't shoot, Terry, old man!' Jared shouted. 'He's had it now. We're safe for some hours at least.'

Emma saw Yolande rush to Jared. She clung to him sobbing hysterically and he put his left arm around her, trying to soothe her.

'Jared darling, has it hurt you?' Yolande cried.

'Only a scratch. I have a first aid kit in the truck. We'll deal with it as soon as we've disposed of this fellow.'

Emma walked slowly towards him. His shirt was nearly ripped from his body and there were ragged claw marks on his brown shoulder that were slowly oozing pinpoints of blood. As she watched, these welled up and became more profuse.

'Have you a clean hanky, Terry?' she asked. He produced one and she made a pad of it. 'Hold on to this,' she ordered. 'You must leave the others to deal with

149

trucking the leopard.'

Jared looked at her as if surprised.

'You seem very calm, Emma,' he observed.

Yolande had stopped crying and clinging to him.

'You can't expect Emma to be as sensitive as I am, Jared, where you're concerned,' she said sharply.

He winced again as if in pain and started to make his way slowly to the truck after he had given some instructions to the others. The leopard, a dead weight now, was carted to the truck and placed in the back where it was well barricaded. Terry took over the driving and Yolande insisted on sitting beside Jared. That left Emma to drive the Land-Rover, accompanied by a rather sobered Craig Mitchell.

'Grand chap, old Jared,' he said expansively to Emma as they drove towards Heron's Creek. 'I guess he just about saved my life.'

Emma nodded. She felt numb with shock.

'He's the only man I've ever thought worthy of my Yolande,' Craig went on. 'I've always said so, and now I've been proved right. He can have her tomorrow as far as I'm concerned. And I can tell you, after this I intend to be very generous with them both. If they want to stay here, I suppose I must put up with it, but I'm hoping like hell that they'll come back with me to Australia.'

Emma hoped so too. For after today she did not want to have Jared living near her. At the moment when the leopard had attacked him, she had suffered a great shock, but it was not fright or terror that had affected her the most, although there had been plenty of that. What had shocked her was the sudden awful realization that she cared for Jared more than words could say. She had always known that he had a physical attraction for her that was hard to resist, but now she knew that she loved him with all her heart. And it was as hopeless as it had been when she was a teenager all those years ago.

CHAPTER TEN

JARED'S wound was treated straight away with the necessary dressings and injections and although the doctor frowned on the idea of him driving himself he was still determined to take the leopard to the luxury game reserve that he had chosen for its new home. It was planned that Terry should drive the truck and Jared should accompany him. They were to start out at dawn of the next day for the journey would take a few hours as the reserve was some couple of hundred miles into Zululand.

Emma had not seen Jared after she had left him at the site of the capture. Perhaps she would appear hard-hearted to him, but she felt that that was the least of her worries. As soon as she had driven Craig back to Heron's Creek and while Jared was still involved with the doctor, she took her small car and drove back to Sunglow, where she occupied herself in supervising the usual chores of the farm and tried to put away from herself the emotional revelation she had suffered. She dined alone not knowing what had happened to Jared. However, later Yolande phoned and told her he was staying there for the night and starting out with Terry the next morning.

'I wanted to go with them, but Jared won't hear of it. He says I should stay and look after Dad. There isn't much wrong with Pa that I can see – at least you wouldn't think so by the amount of whisky he's drunk this evening.'

'How's the leopard?' asked Emma.

'Still unconscious. The vet is coming out first thing to give him an injection which will last until late tomorrow. They've strengthened the bars on the truck, but I tell you, Emma, I'll be glad when all this is over and Jared is safely back here.'

In spite of her resolution not to think about her discovery of her love for Jared, Emma could not help pondering over it when she went to bed that night. Without him across the yard the place seemed very lonely. What would it be like when he had gone for ever as he was bound to do some day? This, she thought, would happen very soon. And perhaps that was all for the best. It had been bad enough concealing from him the physical attraction he held for her, but now that she knew she loved him, the sooner she was rid of him the better.

She found some pills that she had bought for use in case of travel sickness on the plane and took two hoping they would make her sleep. After a while she dozed off and slept until she was startled into wakefulness by a loud knocking on the front door. It was still dark. She looked at the luminous dial of her little clock and saw that it was only four o'clock. Whatever could have happened now? She opened the window and leaned out, calling, 'What is it?'

Jared's voice replied. She could see a dark figure on the verandah below.

'Emma, can you come? Terry's champion cow has started to give birth and I have no one to drive me now. I'm afraid I'll have to ask you to do it. Can you get up and dress? It's a long way, and the sooner we start the better.'

She got up, put on his dressing-gown which was the nearest garment to hand and went down to let him in. She was still heavy with sleep and put her hand to thrust it back from her face. Jared, although his face had been rather grim when she opened the door, smiled at her, saying, 'My dear Emma, that gown becomes you more than it does me, I must say.'

'I don't understand. Why do you want me to come?' she protested.

'There isn't much choice of drivers,' he explained. 'Terry can't come. The doctor says I can't drive because of the scratch on my shoulder. Craig Mitchell is a bit out for the count after his exertions of yesterday. I don't trust Terry's young brothers to drive me, nor have I much faith in Yolande, for that matter – I've had experience of her driving. It's as warm-blooded as her temperament. That, my dear Emma, leaves you.'

'So you think my driving is as cool, calm and collected as me, is that it?'

'Not exactly, but I do know that it's reliable. I'm in a spot, Emma. I know how you feel about me – you've made that plain enough. But at the moment all that matters is disposing of this beast while it's still comatose.'

'Who drove you here?' Emma asked.

'I did, but I wasn't supposed to, and I felt the strain over the last couple of miles.'

Emma sighed. 'All right, I'll come. What will I need?'

'Nothing really. Maybe some washing equipment. I've organized food and coffee already.'

She changed into slacks and a cotton blouse, took up a warm jacket and, after packing a small washbag with toilet things and a lipstick, came down to the truck.

'Good girl! You've been quick. I've given Enoch instructions about the farm work and told Rosie where we're going. We'll be on our way now. I won't be happy until his lordship is in the game reserve.'

Emma took her place in the driver's seat. She was unused to driving a heavy vehicle, but since she had come to the farm she had taken out a heavy duty licence. She would just have to do her best. Jared looked paler than usual.

'How's your shoulder?' she asked.

'No too bad. I'm surviving on painkillers. Just don't get any wild impulses to embrace me without warning as Yolande did, will you?'

153

'You're hopeful!' she laughed shortly. 'That's the last impulse I'm likely to get.'

She felt a surge of pure green-eyed jealousy, but quelled it and concentrated on driving the truck. She would have enough to do today without brooding over her feelings. But why, why, why did everything, every circumstance conspire to throw her into Jared's company?

The road was good and as soon as Emma became used to the truck the driving was not too difficult. Conversation was at a minimum. Emma felt it was not the time or place to start a discussion about his apology or what led up to it. In any case, Jared was drowsy from the painkillers and he slept most of the way.

She glanced across at him once or twice and her heart seemed to flip over because he looked tired and strained, so different from the arrogant, confident man she had both loved and hated. Now she knew that those feelings of hate had gone, in a way she wished they had remained. There could be no future for her with Jared, so why must she feel this tender passion when she looked at his sleeping face that looked gentler and younger than she had ever known it before in spite of his pallor?

They arrived at their destination during the afternoon. It was a private game reserve, more luxurious than the usual government-sponsored ones. It was meant for rich tourists who wanted an experience of wild Africa allied to five-star comforts. But the surroundings looked genuine enough; the thatched huts each with their own bathrooms and air-conditioning were around a main building with a large room furnished with animal trophies and skin rugs but with luxurious, deeply comfortable modern chairs. The brochures advertised 'Dining under the stars' and there was a boma, a fenced enclosure where there were tables and chairs for eating in the open air.

A vet was waiting for them together with the chief game

ranger and they examined the leopard, gave him drugs to rouse him and pronounced him fit to be let free.

'I thought I would have to spend the night in the bush because of the danger to the leopard from hyenas until it regains consciousness,' Jared told Emma, 'but it seems they have enough game wardens and the vet is willing to stay, so that let's me out. They've offered us dinner under the stars just like the brochure says. How will that suit you?'

'I thought we'd be going straight back,' said Emma in surprise

'My dear girl, how could you have got that idea? You can't drive both ways without any rest.'

But when they went to find what accommodation had been allocated to them, the manager smiled awkwardly.

'We thought two men were coming,' he said. 'There's just the one double room. Will that suit? It's a very comfortable room.' His smile became knowing as he glanced from Jared to Emma. 'Otherwise we're completely full. At this time of the year, we always are.'

'That's all right,' said Jared. 'We'll manage, won't we, Emma?'

Emma's brain raced, but she remained speechless while the manager showed them into a spacious room equipped with built-in cupboards, a small fridge, a bathroom en suite, a tawny gold carpet, curtains printed with figures of animals and, in the centre of all this comfort, a low double bed that looked big enough, thought Emma, to accommodate six people. She waited until the manager had departed. His grin seemed to linger in the air like the Cheshire cat's smile in Alice in Wonderland. Then she turned furiously upon Jared.

'You knew this was going to happen!' she accused. 'You planned it on purpose. Well, let me tell you I won't have it at any price. If you intend to sleep here, I'll sleep in the bath. How could you possibly accept this room?

You're the most smug, conceited man I've ever met!'

His laugh of genuine amusement infuriated her still further.

'How dare you think you could deliberately put me in a position like this and that I would accept it meekly? You have the most terribly inflated opinion of your own charms, Jared, but they don't have the effect on me that you would wish!' she finished.

Jared was still laughing and, walking towards her, put his good arm around her shoulders. She was so beside herself with rage by this time that she swung round and caught him a glancing blow on the face. He seized both wrists, still stronger than she was in spite of his disabled shoulder, and forced her down upon the bed, pinioning her there so that she could not move.

'What a tiger cat! Give me the leopard any day.'

She was trembling with rage, struggling to get free from the iron grip on her wrists.

'Let me go, do you hear? I hate you, Jared, I hate you more than anyone I've ever met! And if you think I'm going to sleep with you in this room tonight, you're very much mistaken!'

He laughed again, but the dark gleam in his eyes was dangerous.

'Who said anything about sleep?' he drawled. 'I have no intention of sleeping while you're around, my golden, beautiful Emma.'

'If you don't let me go, I'm going to scream for help! I've got a loud voice when I want to be heard,' she threatened.

'And who do you expect to come to your rescue? Not our leering manager, that's certain. And we're far away from the other guests. That's one of the beauties of staying in a luxury camp. Don't you know the brochure offers peace and tranquillity completely on your own with your loved one? Ideal for honeymoons!'

He released her at last and stood looking down at her with his dark vital gaze that seemed to penetrate the secrets of her mind.

'My lovely Emma, I admit I was at fault that morning, but it won't happen again,' he said softly. 'I've told you that I'll never force you to anything you don't want to do. I'll go now and leave you to get ready for dinner. When you've had that boma under the stars routine, perhaps you may be in a more receptive mood.'

He walked out and Emma was left to mull over his words. Was he teasing her? she wondered. She wanted to believe this, but could not forget the expression of his eyes as he had held her down on the bed. She was shaken and trembling with fury rather than with fright. How could I have possibly thought I loved him? she thought. I don't now, that's certain. How with all my previous experience of his opportunism, could I have let myself in for this situation? And what am I to do? Anyhow, I can't come to any harm by having dinner with him if the hotel is as full as the manager says it is. There'll be plenty of other people around.

The atmosphere of the open-air dining-room was very exotic, very African. Flat-topped thorn trees formed a natural roof and from the branches hung large gold paper lanterns. The tablecloths were of gay African prints and the old miners' lamps gave light at each table, which was hidden from its neighbours by a screen of handwoven rushes. The effect was far too intimate to suit Emma's present mood.

He was waiting there for her, his dark profile clean-cut against the light basketwork design of the screen, his hair glossy as a starling's wing. He got up quickly and took her hands in his.

'Emma, are you still cross with me?' he asked gently. 'Forget it, my dear, and enjoy your dinner. Not to worry – I intend to sleep in the van. I know when I'm not wanted.

'I've given instructions that it should be cleaned of all traces of our guest and they're providing me with a mattress. You can sleep peacefully on your own now. Will that suit you?'

She nodded, not knowing what reply to make. Was he lulling her into a false sense of security? she wondered. And did he hope that the dinner and wine in this lovely setting would work the miracle that he had not been able to achieve himself? If this was so she must show him clearly that he was mistaken.

There was a hum of light conversation around them, but they were so screened off from the other occupants of the tables that they might have been on their own. Soft music flowed over the warm air and the scent of stephanotis wafted around the enclosure like a white lovely ghost.

Jared ordered a light sparkling wine.

'It's almost as harmless as I am,' he assured Emma.

'Then I'd better leave it alone,' she said.

Her eyes were drawn to his and she wondered how she could find herself held by some desperate enchantment of the senses when she wanted to be withdrawn and sensible? What combination of features made him appear to be everything she had ever wanted in a man? She had known men more handsome than he was, and younger too, nearer to her own age, so why, in spite of everything, when he gently touched her hand as he did now did her heart rock with joy?

'You think too much, my Emma – I've told you so before. Enjoy your fresh asparagus, which was doubtless brought here at immense cost to the management and the guests, and taste your beautiful trout that was swimming in a nearby stream only this morning.'

Emma noticed that, although Jared encouraged her to eat, he took very little himself. The delicious savoury venison dish was hardly touched and he brushed aside the waiter's piled trolley of sweet puddings, apricot bavarois, cassata and chocolate mousse. But he drank two cups of black coffee.

'Won't that keep you awake, Jared?' Emma asked.

'I don't think I'm going to get much sleep anyway,' he confessed. 'This scratch has started making itself felt.'

'Have you still got some painkillers?' she asked.

'A few. I'll manage. Don't worry, Emma. All I need is rest.'

'You can have my bed and I'll sleep in the truck,' she offered.

'Good heavens, no! I've slept in much worse places in my time. I'll be quite all right by morning.'

He took her to the door of her room and when she turned on her light she saw that beneath his tan his skin had an ashen look. But again he brushed aside her attempts to persuade him to take her bed.

'If you need me . . . I mean if you don't feel well later on, please call me,' she said hesitantly.

'Take care, Emma,' he smiled. 'I might hold you to that!'

Unexpectedly he took her hand and kissed it, and she was alarmed to feel that his skin as it brushed against her felt hot and dry.

'Good night, Emma. We'd better make an early start.'

Left alone, she felt restless and worried about Jared. She must occupy herself in some way to keep her mind off him, so she decided to wash her blouse. It was drip-dry and that at least would be clean for the return journey. She took her time washing it, hung it up to dry, then came back into the room and lay on top of the bed, still in her slacks and her lacy bra. She kept thinking she must rouse herself to get up and undress and get under the sheets, but she felt too drowsy to stir from the comfort of resting after the cares and hazards of the long day. There was only one small bedside lamp still burning and soon she fell asleep without carrying out her intention.

She was aroused from a deep sleep by the sound of urgent tapping. For a moment she could not recall where she was, asleep in a strange room and clad still in denim slacks and a bra. She looked at her watch. It was past midnight. It could only be Jared, and as she realized this she heard his voice.

'Emma, are you awake? I need some help.'

Without even thinking of her appearance, she went to the door and opened it. Jared stood there, his face flushed, his dark eyes glittering. She stepped back as he came into the room.

'This damn scratch is giving me hell, Emma. I've brought some more dressings, but I can't manage it on my own. Do you think you can do it? You aren't the fainting kind, are you?'

She helped him take off his shirt and carefully undid the bandage.

'What does it look like?' he asked.

Horrible, she wanted to say, but she reassured him. It was inflamed but not septic. She thought it needed another dressing, and proceeded to do this.

'You're surprisingly competent, Emma,' he remarked when she had finished. 'As well as remarkably beautiful.'

For the first time she became aware that she had done all this for him while in a very advanced state of undress.

'I . . . I washed my blouse and then I fell asleep on the bed,' she explained hastily.

'Don't apologize,' he said ruefully. 'A bikini would reveal more. You look very lovely. I only wish I were in a better state to appreciate it.'

You mean to take advantage of it, she thought, but did not say so. She wondered whether their scene before dinner had made his shoulder worse. He took her hand in his and kissed each finger separately. His face was hotter than it had been before.

'You'd better stay here,' she said. 'I can't let you go back to the truck.'

Jared laughed ruefully.

'I think it must be the first time I've ever been invited to stay the night with a woman for reasons of my health! All right, Emma, I'm glad to accept the invitation. My wretched scratch will take the place of the drawn sword between us.'

He had taken another pill and, lying on the bed, he was soon asleep. Emma covered him with a blanket and then carefully took up her place on the other side of the wide bed. She lay awake for a long time listening to his ragged breathing. If he became worse, she would have to call for help, she thought, but gradually it seemed to become more regular and at last she fell into an uneasy doze.

She had meant to wake during the night, but the first streaks of dawn were yellow in the eastern sky when she opened her eyes. She must have slept more deeply in the last couple of hours, for Jared had rolled over to her side during the night and his head was against her bare shoulder. His face was cool now and he looked rested and peaceful. She shifted a little, trying to make him come into a more comfortable position, and he opened his eyes. Their faces were so close on the pillow that they almost touched.

'I've never had a more pleasant awakening,' he murmured. He cupped her chin in his hand and looked intently into her eyes. 'It was very sweet of you to let me stay here, Emma.'

He kissed her softly and the truth blazed out at her again, as it had when he faced the leopard. Heart, mind and body, she was his. It was useless to try to deceive herself otherwise. She got up from the bed and went into the bathroom to retrieve her blouse, buttoned it carefully and approached the bed again.

'Shall I ring for coffee?' she asked.

'I can think of nothing I'd appreciate more, except perhaps ... oh, well, let it pass. But, Emma, don't you mind that everyone in the hotel will know you've had me in the room all night?' he asked curiously.

'It was my own decision,' she said. 'Are you really feeling better, Jared?'

'Magnificent! Isn't there some belief that it rejuvenates old men to have a young girl sleep in their bed? You must have passed on some magic to me, Emma.'

The magic of love, she thought, but how could that be, since they had slept all night side by side as innocently as children?

'Are you calling yourself an old man, Jared?' she asked. 'Then I must start taking your temperature, because I've never heard you say that before.'

'Hardly old, but I can give you seventeen years, Emma. And last night I felt about ninety. But today I feel as young as you are.'

Rose-coloured clouds were heralding the light as they set off half an hour later. Emma drove slowly, for they were still in the game reserve and it was as if they had come into some magic world beyond the reach of time. Russet-coloured impala frolicked in the early light, butting each other playfully and stopping to stare at the truck as they walked softly and secretly to the waterhole. Birds called with clear notes from the flat thorn trees and stately waterbuck paused to stand still as a stone and watch the progress of the vehicle. A black-backed jackal intent on his search for insects did not notice them at all. He looked as pretty as a fox with his gold coat caught by the early sun.

How happy I am, thought Emma, driving with my love. But then she thought, he's not my love. If he's anybody's love he belongs to Yolande. He can't know how I feel about him and I shall take good care he never does know. She wished they could stay together in this enchanting unreal world, where wild scents of Africa made the pulses tremble and the animals, leading their secret lives in the blossoming forest, were so perfect and beautiful that they seemed like a mediaeval painting.

When they came out of the game reserve, she felt a pang of regret that she was leaving all that strange world behind. But the enchantment persisted in her mind as they drove along the main road, with sweeping, sloping lands of green sugar cane turning to silver in the wind and moving like waves of the sea. They came in the afternoon into more familiar country, a land of sparse grass and rocks, small green thorn trees and hillsides with the strange shapes of aloes and euphorbia marching over them. The journey was almost over. They were coming home – home, with its problems and with Yolande at Heron's Creek, ready and willing to claim Jared as her own.

'You can leave me at Heron's Creek, Emma,' said Jared as if reading her thoughts. 'I said I'd look in there on my way back – Craig has some problems he wants me to settle. You can phone if you have any worries, but I'm sure Enoch will have coped while we've been away. He can drive the truck over tomorrow. I'll probably stay the night there.'

To Emma it seemed as if someone had thrust her under a cold shower. Absurd that she had felt he had enjoyed her company today. As soon as they were back he was rushing off to Yolande. And she was to be left alone.

The next morning the phone rang very early and she rushed to it, her heart pounding, her body quivering, her whole being tremulous at the idea of hearing his voice. But he sounded distant and very far away. One always had to be cautious on these party lines, but surely he was taking this to extremes.

'Emma, good morning. I trust you slept well. Look, something has come up. Craig Mitchell isn't at all well and feels incapable of running the farm at the moment. You've told me often enough that you want to have a go at managing Sunglow on your own, so here's your chance. I know you won't miss me. If you need any advice or help you only have to phone, but I daresay Terry will be there often enough, and you can always appeal to the Citrus Board to send someone out to advise you.'

'But, Jared ... you mean you don't intend to come back?' she said anxiously.

'Yes, that's just what I do mean. I'll tell Mr. Johnson about it. But, Emma – after all, it's what you'd always wanted, isn't it? Now tell me you're delighted with my decision.'

Emma, her heart somewhere down in her boots, her whole body trembling, tried desperately to summon up a natural voice.

'You must do as you think best, Jared. It was just that it seems such a sudden decision. As you say, I'll probably manage well enough on my own. I won't be without advice.'

But I'll be without you, she thought, as she turned slowly away from the phone. Why had he done this to her? It wasn't just on account of Craig Mitchell's health, she was sure. He must want to be in close proximity to Yolande. Perhaps she had been annoyed about their trip to the game reserve and had decided to get Jared away from Emma and have him all to herself. And she had succeeded only too well.

CHAPTER ELEVEN

THE weeks passed and Emma flung herself into the work of the farm with an urgency born of desperation. The orchards needed constant watching and had to be sprayed with powders and liquids to protect the ripening fruit from the insects, fungi and diseases that preyed on it. From darkest green the oranges swelled and ripened gradually through shades of lemon yellow to flaming gold. When she went out in the early morning to give her instructions to the workers, the dew was on the grass and the trees with their dark green leaves and ripening lamps of fruit looked like an orchard in the Garden of the Hesperides where apples of purest gold hung on the branches.

Emma was hardworking and her employees came to respect her and to listen to her requests, and, if she became puzzled, her problems were disentangled by appealing to the officials of the Citrus Board as they came around visiting the farms regularly. It was not in that direction that she missed Jared. It was in her own heart. When he had come for his belongings, she had deliberately gone out and left Rosie to meet him and see to his requirements. He must have taken this as an indication that she did not want anything further to do with him, for she had had no communication from him at all since then.

She was leading the life of a recluse. She refused Terry's invitations, worked all day, including the weekends, and did not even go into the town. If anything was needed she sent Enoch in with a list of shopping. And she fell into bed at night and slept a dreamless sleep until first light when she got up, took a flask of coffee and some sandwiches and went down to the orchards to see what needed doing that day. But sometimes in the evening after her light supper, when Rosie had gone to her room and she was left alone, she would take her coffee out to the swing seat and sit in the blue of the balmy African night, hearing the pulsating sound of guitars from the workers' compound. Then thoughts of Jared would flutter into her mind like white doves finding their home again and she would feel an agonizing sense of loss for something she had never really possessed.

By March, the great heat, that had prevailed from after Christmas and had helped to ripen the fruit, began to diminish somewhat. Clear sunlit days were followed by nights with a touch of chill, like a sparkling glass of champagne that has been subtly iced to exactly the right temperature. The cool nights were needed to bring the fruit to its right colour. Emma was looking forward to the harvest now which would begin in April. She had already arranged about extra pickers, but packing fortunately was not her responsibility. The oranges, when they were harvested, would be taken to a central packing house and sorted by skilled workers.

At last the time came when her adviser from the Citrus Board judged that the fruit should be picked. Emma felt almost afraid to start, for the oranges seemed to have taken so long to reach this stage and, after all the spraying and fertilizing over the long months, it was most important that they should be picked very carefully and that nothing should go wrong. Terry came along to see her at that time and confirmed the fact that the fruit was ripe enough.

'I wish I could give you more help,' he said, 'but I'm up to the eyes in it myself. You know, one orange tree can carry as many as fifteen hundred oranges, and you must see that each one is cut carefully from the tree.'

Emma was quite confident that she could manage it on her own. She found that she got on well with the coloured workers and they seemed eager to please her. The Africans had a pet name for her that meant 'The girl with the red hair'. She took on extra workers and decided to start straight away. For weeks the weather had been set fair and showed no signs of breaking. It was a busy time. She worked all day supervising the gathering of the crop. The pickers wore gloves so that the fruit would not be harmed in handling. Ever so gently the gleaming golden oranges were placed in a bag hanging from the picker's shoulder. These bags had a special method of opening at the bottom so that their contents could be gently released into trailers which would later take the fruit to the pack-houses.

Emma learned to do it herself and worked away with the best of them. She supervised the preparation of food for the many workers and she and Rosie were kept at it from morning until night.

On the fifth day, the picking was well under way. Emma reckoned there would only be another two days' work and then it would all be over. She looked forward to a time when she could relax and rest, for the last few weeks had been the hardest she had ever known. That morning she rose early. For the last weeks the mornings had been the best part of the day, crisp and clear, with large intricate spiders' webs hanging dew-laden between the ragged chrysanthemums. But this morning there was a change in the atmosphere. Instead of being fresh and cold with a dawn breeze, the air was warm and still. There was a clammy close feeling and it seemed an effort to accomplish anything as strenuous as picking the fruit. When the sun had risen, it blazed down as if it were mid-December instead of April, and the coloured assistants went for frequent drinks of cold tea and washed their hot faces and arms with the hose.

Enoch, Emma's foreman, shook his head, saying, 'There's bad weather coming.'

'What kind of bad weather?' asked Emma.

'Hard to say, ma'am. Perhaps a storm. But it may pass over.'

The hot conditions seemed to slow down the picking and by noon great white cumulus clouds started to build up, raising their heads like giant presences from behind the mountains. They climbed up across the sky, piling up in swirling thunderheads. It seemed certain now that something unusual was happening. Emma felt anxious. She had no experience of bad weather here, except for that one summer storm on Christmas Day, but this felt different. That had been a torrential downpour of rain soon over, but something about the feel of the weather was odd and not the same as the previous storm.

She had gone back to the house when the workers stopped for their lunch break. They had to have a rest, however anxious she was to see the fruit gathered before the storm broke, since they had been working since early dawn. She was eating a sandwich and drinking orange juice while watching the enormous clouds overhead. From white they had changed to a grey swirling mass, changing formation until it was quite dizzying to the eye and below great loops of greyish-green cloud hung down in curious shapes. As she watched, a truck drew up in front of the verandah and her heart missed a beat as she saw a tall figure jump out and stride swiftly towards her. Jared! What could have brought him here? He frowned as he came towards her. He looked anything but pleased to see her again, she thought.

'Emma, what are you doing here?' he demanded. 'Who's supervising the picking?'

'I am, of course, but it's their lunch break and mine too, Jared.'

'Emma, are you mad?' he snapped. 'There's a hailstorm heading straight for you and you talk calmly of a lunch break!'

'A hailstorm?' she queried.

'For God's sake, can't you see it? Those clouds are a sure sign.'

'But ... but ... Enoch just said bad weather ... he didn't know.'

'We aren't supposed to be in the hail belt here,' he said. 'Enoch's young and and hasn't any experience of it. But it's there and it's coming fast. Get into the house and I'll go and see to your workers. They must get a move on. Any fruit that's left will be mashed to a pulp. Even if the hail isn't hard, the fruit will be pitted and unfit for sale. I've brought more pickers from Heron's Creek. I dropped them at the orchards and I've already told your workers to get on with it. There's not a moment to be lost. I'll go down there now and try to get them going quickly. You get into the house and close all the windows. It's a frightening experience when it strikes.'

'I'm not afraid, Jared. It's my harvest and I'm coming with you. If there's any danger, I'll face it too.'

He smiled, and to Emma it was as if the sun had appeared in a gap through all the threatening, swirling cloud.

'Obstinate redheaded woman, come on, then!'

They were working against time, struggling to gather in the rest of the harvest in frightful conditions. A howling gale whipped around the trees, bowing them this way and that and making the picking extremely difficult.

'What about the crop at Heron's Creek?' gasped Emma as she encountered Jared in their mad scramble to finish all the trees.

'We completed the picking yesterday, fortunately for the Mitchells. It's their crop this year.'

'How did you know it might strike here?' asked Emma.

'Because the only times we've had hail before it's followed a certain course and Sunglow has usually been the victim. Now stop talking and let's get on.'

They could not hope to save all the crop, but a good part of what remained was in the sheds by the time the storm struck. At the first sign of rain, Jared ordered the workers to run for it and he hustled Emma towards the homestead. But before they could get across the yard large chunks of ice started hurtling down from the skies and they were forced to take shelter in the old museum. The light was lurid now, an eerie green, and there was no lamp in the place, as Rosie had taken it to refill it and forgotten to bring it back in Jared's absence.

Faster and faster came the hail until there seemed nothing in all the world but the drumming of huge pieces of ice upon the corrugated iron roof of the building. It was like being in a bombardment. They could scarcely see across the room, for it was almost as dark as night with a weird green luminous light that no night ever had. The narrow verandah in front of the building sheltered the windows from the hail, but huge jagged blocks cannonaded down upon the wooden floor of the outside porch.

Jared had taken no further notice of Emma when they had come inside but stood at the window watching the storm. He seemed almost to be enjoying it, thought Emma, resentfully watching the tall figure that was blocking out the light still further. She sat on the bed and put her hands over her ears, but she could not block out the dreadful dinning noise overhead. With a rending crack one of the panes of glass shattered and the curtain blew out in the icy gale that seemed to whip around the room. She went over to Jared to help pick up the pieces of glass, but she was trembling so much that she was hard put to it to gather them up without cutting herself.

'Let me do it, Emma, for God's sake. You may be good at some things, but you're useless at this.'

She was tired out and cold, and his sharp tone seemed the finishing touch to the afternoon.

'It's stupid for either of us to do it while there's so little light!' she shouted, scarcely able to make herself heard.

He had touched her hand by accident as they both grovelled on the floor for the broken glass.

'You're frozen, girl. Come over here and I'll wrap you in a blanket.'

He made her sit on the bed against a pillow with her feet up and wrapped her around in a red blanket that was printed with black leopards.

'How appropriate,' she remarked, but he could not hear because of the thunder of the hail on the roof. He sat beside her on the bed and put his arm around her, and Emma was glad of his support. It felt so comforting to have him here, not to have to worry any more about bringing in the harvest on her own. He would be gone very soon, she supposed, but for this little while he was hers and she could realize how much she had missed him. He did not attempt to kiss her. I suppose all that's over, she thought, however little it meant to him. He's been with Yolande so long that even he doesn't want anyone else. She glanced at him and saw with a throb of the pulses how his bright blue shirt was open so that the healed scar showed upon his shoulder. His dark hair was ruffled, damp and curling, and there was the smell of new grass about him, mysterious, alluring, utterly characteristic of Jared.

The sound of the hail that had been like a bombardment had eased and was only a small fusillade of light shots. He got up from his place beside her.

'It's almost over now,' he said from the window. 'We'll be able to get out and assess the damage in a little while. As soon as we've gone over the place, I must get back to Heron's Creek and see what's happened there.'

'How are they?' asked Emma. 'I haven't seen Yolande for ages.'

'She's all involved with planning her twenty-first

birthday party. It's going to be quite an occasion. She's asking the whole district and some Australian friends who happen to be around now. Doubtless you will get an invitation in due course. I suppose you'll come with Terry?' he added.

'I expect so,' Emma agreed.

He disentangled her from the blanket and lifted her to stand up again. She swayed and he caught her against him, and for a moment she felt again the whole hard strength of his lithe body. But he quickly put her aside.

'Go back to the house, Emma, and I'll look for Enoch. I'll send him back to report to you, when we've finished looking around. I must get back to Heron's Creek afterwards.'

I've hardly spoken to him, thought Emma sadly. But she said calmly, 'Thank you, Jared, for your help. I'm very grateful.'

She watched his tall slim figure recede into the distance. He only came because it was an emergency; when shall I see him again? she wondered.

She spent the next few days helping to clear up the damage that the hail had done. Leaves had been stripped from the trees. The lucerne which was to be the winter feed for the cattle had been flattened into the ground. The small area of land that was used for vegetables was a morass of ruined plants, and the garden at the back of the house was in a similar condition.

Terry came over to give Emma advice and to view the damage.

'So long as you've got the crop in, that's all right,' he told her. 'These other things don't matter so much. You'll be amazed how quickly the battered plants recover when they've had a bit of sun.'

She accepted Terry's offer to drive her into town in his truck to get new vegetable seeds and seed potatoes. This was the first time she had been to town for a long time and she dressed carefully in her cream slacks suit with an apricot blouse that contrasted well with her brighter hair. In every shop she entered, people asked her about the hailstorm. Emma was surprised by the amount of sympathy and friendliness she encountered and she began to feel that she was becoming part of the community.

She met Terry for lunch in the hotel and while they were having a drink, she noticed a rather noisy crowd on the other side of the courtyard.

'Isn't that Yolande?' she asked Terry, for she could see a glimpse of silver-blonde hair.

'Yes, she's with her Australian friends. They're staying at Heron's Creek, I believe.'

Is Jared going to join them? Emma wondered, and was distressed by the way her heart thudded at the idea of seeing him, but although they were there for some while, Jared did not appear. Later as she was going out of the foyer of the hotel after lunch and Terry had gone for the truck, she had a brief encounter with Yolande, who was on her own as well. She was looking very lovely in a slacks suit of palest blue that emphasized the silver shade of her hair and fitted her slender figure to perfection.

'Emma! I haven't seen you for a million years. What have you been doing with yourself?' she asked.

'Running the farm,' Emma replied.

'You're a demon for work, aren't you?' commented Yolande. 'I've been meaning to phone you about my twenty-first. You and Terry can come, can't you? It's in two weeks' time on Saturday. We're going to make a big do of it. We've hired a special band from the city and a caterer. You see, it's not only my twenty-first – we're going to make it a double occasion. I'll tell you about it later, but I must fly now. My car's running out of meter time and Dad has a fit at the number of traffic fines I get each month. Be seeing you!'

Away she fled, a picture of liveliness and joy. Emma walked slowly to the truck. So now she knew for certain. Jared and Yolande were going to announce that they were to be married. But she had known it would happen. It should not be such a blow. She should not feel as if her world was ending, for that world she had dreamed of had never really begun.

'You're very quiet,' Terry said on their way back.

'Sorry. Yolande asked us to her twenty-first party in two weeks' time,' Emma told him.

'I'll look forward to that. You did say we could go, I suppose? You don't mind coming with me?'

'Oh, Terry, of course not!'

She was touched by his humbleness where she was concerned. He was like a large friendly boxer dog who wasn't quite sure of his welcome.

When she arrived home and Terry had left her, Rosie came bustling in as if she had something of importance to say.

'You must phone Mr. Jared straight away, Miss Emma. He phoned to ask for you twice. He says it's urgent.'

Emma hesitated at the phone. What could Jared have to say to her? Why had he phoned twice? He came on to the line straight away. As he said 'Hello', his low, black velvet voice triggered off a throbbing pulse somewhere below her diaphragm, but it was succeeded by a flash of anger as he said sharply, 'Emma, where the hell have you been all morning? I thought you spent your life on the farm?'

'This morning I happened to go into town with Terry. Have you any objection?'

'Nothing to do with me, of course. Just wondered where you could have got to. No need to make a big scene about it.'

Emma had difficulty in controlling her temper.

'It's you, Jared, who's making the big scene,' she retorted. 'What have you phoned me for? To tell me I shouldn't go in to town?'

'All right, calm down, Emma. Forget the redheaded temperament for once. I phoned to ask you to come up to see the dam with me. I've had it fixed and it concerns both our farms, so you'd better come and see it. Will tomorrow suit you?'

Emma thought quickly.

'Yes, all right. Where is this dam?'

'Some way up the mountain in the forest. I'll bring a small truck.'

'Is . . . is anyone else coming?' she asked.

'No, Emma. Now don't start being spinsterish. This is a business date, nothing else. Understand?'

'I'll keep you to that,' Emma snapped, and put down the receiver.

'I'm going to see the dam with Mr. Jared tomorrow,' she told Rosie.

Rosie beamed.

'Why not ask him back to dinner, Miss Emma, and then I can cook properly. I'll roast that piece of beef and do Yorkshire pudding and roast potatoes and . . .'

'No, Rosie, I can't ask him for dinner,' protested Emma.

'Why not? He doesn't get roast potatoes like mine at Heron's Creek. That Miss Yolande, she doesn't even eat potatoes.'

'I don't think Miss Yolande would want him to come to dinner with us, Rosie, and I don't think he would want to come either.'

Rosie started to go back to the kitchen, shaking her head, but in the doorway she made her parting shot.

'Mr. Jared's a man . . . *ndoda* . . . you won't get another like him. Why you let Miss Yolande take him right from under your nose, Miss Emma?'

Oh, Rosie, I never had him, so there wasn't any taking away, thought Emma. She was thrilled and yet terrified at the idea of driving alone with Jared to inspect the dam. But she must be sensible. He had not even sounded as if he wanted to see her. It was purely a business meeting, as he had pointed out.

When he came next morning, it was hard to conceal her joy. It would take an hour or two, he had told her, and she resolved to herself that she must not spoil it by quarrelling with him, for it was probably the last time she would see him alone before he became formally Yolande's prospective husband.

'You look sixteen,' he said, smiling at her as he helped her up into the high cab of the truck. Why did his touch have this overwhelming effect on her? she wondered. She had never had this glowing experience with any other man. It was quite maddening that it should happen with him.

She had dressed in blue denim jeans and a blue striped blouse and her hair was tied back in a ponytail with a dark blue bow almost the same colour as her eyes, but small tendrils escaped and curled around her brows. She sat in the side of the struck, leaving a gap of about two feet between them. Jared must have noticed this, but merely smiled and made no comment. Emma's whole body felt tense and strung up. She tried hard to relax. It was too stupid to feel like this just because she was driving with Jared. He began to talk about ordinary things, the farm, the damage the hailstorm had done, the animals, and very slowly her tension eased until by the time they came to the forest gate she was talking naturally and even beginning to enjoy the drive through country she had not seen before.

The forests were on the side of the mountain and the dam was further up in a hollow formed by two hills. It was natural forest with huge old trees, oak and yellow-wood with some pines, but a wide drive had been cut through it by the forest rangers for use by their trucks and also as a firebreak. They drove along under an overhanging canopy of giant trees, and Emma would have liked to stop and look more closely at these, but she thought it would be better not to suggest this. Sunlight shone in radiant shafts through the leaves, dappling the ground with patterns of light and shade, and the ground itself was thick with green moss and the carpet of leaves and pine needles that was brown now from the summer's heat. Here and there huge rocks stood like prehistoric dwellings, and lichen and Spanish moss hung from the trees.

But soon they emerged from the trees and began to climb a winding path on the side of the mountain. On one side there was a steep drop, and Emma wondered what they would do if they encountered another vehicle coming in the opposite direction, but this did not happen, and when they stood at last above the wall of the small dam it seemed to her as if they could have been the last people alive in the world.

It was so still. Only the rustle of grass and the gentle murmur of rock doves broke the silence. Far below the valley stretched to the horizon with farmlands dotted with thorn trees and grass that was turning brown in the autumn weather. A train like a toy curved busily towards the horizon, and the town with its white houses looked like an architect's model.

'We'll have to get down to the bottom of the dam wall to inspect the work they've done on it,' said Jared.

They scrambled down, and Emma could not avoid taking the hand he offered in the rough places. At last they stood below the wall and he explained how the cracks had been filled and the place reinforced.

'Both of our farms have water pipes leading from here,' he told her. 'It's something we have in common. Mac left provision for his half of the repairs. I suppose Mr. Johnson told you about it.'

She tried to take an intelligent interest in his conversation, but all the time she was aware of his hand on her arm, his mouth, that mouth that had kissed her and had thrilled her even when it had been against her wishes, so close she could have touched it. She turned aside and swayed perilously on the edge of the bank where they were standing overlooking the dam wall. He put out his hands from behind her and caught her to him, and, even when he had steadied her, he did not let her go but went on holding her, his face against her hair.

'My obstinate, redheaded Emma, it's been a long time, hasn't it, since we were alone together?'

Her body thrilled in tremulous ecstasy as she felt his arms around her once more.

'Lovely one, what am I to do about you?' he whispered. 'Every time I set eyes on you I desire you.'

She knew that if she turned around they would be in each other's arms and he would kiss her, the gentle kisses that could so quickly change to caresses of overwhelming fire. For a moment as she stood with his hands pressing the curve of her waist and his mouth moving against her cheek, she was violently tempted, tempted to turn around and say, 'Take me, Jared, I'm yours. I always have been. What does it matter if you belong to another woman? Let us delight in this strange enchantment of the senses that we both feel, even if with you it could only be for today.'

But what would follow? A loneliness more bitter than she had ever known before. He intended to marry Yolande however much Emma attracted him. She saw herself back at the farm, alone and ashamed that she had followed her own fervent desires when to him she was only a passing fancy that would soon disappear when he was married to someone else.

She took his hands from her body and walked away from him towards the car. She tried to speak firmly.

'This is a business trip, Jared. You said so, remember?'

His hands had fallen to his sides and he looked at her for a long time, examining every inch of her, almost, she thought, as if he were trying to commit her to memory. Then he laughed, a sound that had no joy in it.

'So I did, Emma. You're right as usual. Shall we go?'

She, who was often at a loss for words with him, found herself chattering nervously the whole of the way back, as if she were trying to efface the desperate emotion she had felt on the quiet slopes of the mountain. But Yolande's name was never mentioned between them.

CHAPTER TWELVE

HER whole inclination was to phone Yolande and say she could not go to the party, but she hesitated to let Terry down. Finally she decided that she must go through with it. It was no good running away from something that after all she had known for a long time was bound to happen. During the day she tried sometimes successfully to banish him from her thoughts, but at night, before she went to sleep, Jared's face would flash on to the screen of her mind and she would attempt in vain to forget that mobile passionate mouth and the expression of his eyes when he looked at her.

With a feeling of pride she decided that she must buy herself a new dress and try to look her loveliest on that night. 'I'll go down with all flags flying,' she thought, and then laughed because she was being so ridiculous. Whoever would notice what she looked like on Yolande's important night? Nevertheless she must do this just to satisfy herself.

She went shopping in a small boutique in the little town, wanting something that would make her look completely the opposite of the everyday young girl in denim jeans, and she found a warm russet velvet dress with simple beautiful lines. It clung to her slim waist and fluted out into a bell-shaped skirt, and the neck was low-cut, flattering her creamy neck and the alluring curve of her breasts.

'It's your dress,' the shop owner told her. 'It seems as if it was made for you. You couldn't do better. It makes your hair look absolutely gorgeous, and aren't you lucky to have such a lovely fair skin? You don't look as if the sun affects you at all.'

It was true that unlike most redheads, Emma had a creamy alabaster skin that could take extremes of climate. She bought a new becoming apricot-coloured make-up that gave her usually pale skin a radiant glow, and, on the day of the party, she had her hair styled in a more sophisticated fashion, swept across her head in soft loose waves. She had a topaz pendant that had been left to her by her grandmother and this, worn on a gold chain, seemed a perfect accessory for her velvet dress.

The evenings were crisp and cool now with a warning of the coming winter, and Rosie had put a match to the fire and brought in the tray of drinks without even being asked.

'If you won't have Mr. Jared,' she said to Emma, 'you had better take Mr. Terry. He is a good man and you need a husband.'

'I don't think I do, Rosie. I can manage perfectly well by myself.'

Rosie gave a scornful snort and went out of the room. But Terry was late. He phoned and explained very apologetically that he had been held up by some crisis on the farm.

'Won't be long, Emma. We'll enjoy it all the more when we get there, won't we? Have a drink while you're waiting for me. It'll put you in the right mood.'

Would it? thought Emma. She poured herself a glass of sherry that was the same colour as her dress, and sat sipping it slowly and gazing into the fire. Would she ever get over this yearning for Jared? she wondered. Her mistake had been to accept his presence on the farm in the first place. She should have known that he would continue to attract her more and more in spite of all her efforts to resist his charm. Suppose she were to marry Terry? Would that solve her problem? When Jared married Yolande – no, from this very night when he became engaged to her, she, Emma, would have to make every effort to put him right out of her mind. Suppose she went away? But she loved the farm. She loved this country. It was her life now. She did not want to change it.

Terry arrived to interrupt her thoughts. He looked clean and spruce and healthy with his fresh complexion, his spotless white shirt and dark suit.

'Putting on weight a bit,' he admitted, patting his diaphragm. 'Haven't worn a dress suit for months, but this is a very special occasion, isn't it?'

The party was in full swing when they came to Heron's Creek. Africans with torches were directing the cars to the parking area and, because they were late, Terry and Emma had quite a long way to go.

'I guess I should have left you at the house before coming here,' said Terry as he switched off the engine, 'but I wanted to ask you something and I think I may have more courage in the dark.'

Emma wanted to say, whatever it is, Terry, don't ask me now. After her session of dreaming beside the fire, and knowing that she was so soon to see him, the presence of Jared was all around her. She could not fling it aside.

'I guess you know what I want to say,' he went on. 'Perhaps I should have waited until the end of the evening. Maybe that would be more romantic. But I'm no good at this sort of thing, Emma. You look so terrific tonight, I can't keep quiet about it any longer. Don't you think it would be a good idea if you were to marry me, Emma? I'm crazy about you, and that's a fact.'

Emma put out her hand and took his large one in her own. 'Terry,' she said gently, 'I don't think it would be a good idea. I'm sorry – I like you very much, I'm very fond of you, but not in that way.'

'How do you know? I think you're great. I've never felt like this about any other girl before. Emma dear, give it a try,' he pleaded. 'Say we can become engaged at least. We get on so well together.'

'Yes, we do, but . . .' There seemed no way to explain her predicament to him. She could not tell him she was in love with a man who belonged to someone else. 'Let's go in, Terry,' she finished.

'Think about it, Emma. I guess I shouldn't have rushed you. Perhaps by the end of the evening you may change your mind. Engagements are catching, they say, and Yolande seems all set for announcing hers.'

When they were quite a distance from the house, they could hear the sound of music floating on the still air. The large living rooms had been cleared for dancing and there was the sound of laughter and conversation from the patio. There was an autumnal fragrance of chrysanthemums and wood smoke, but here the air was still warm. The stones seemed to retain their golden noonday heat and the guests were sitting there oblivious of the slight chill that had been evident at Sunglow. The windows were all open to the night, and Emma stood at an open doorway like a child looking in at a Christmas festival.

Jared was there dancing with Yolande. She was smiling up at him, dressed in a sophisticated black dress with tiny shoulder straps of diamanté. She was looking absolutely beautiful and, as Emma watched, she saw Jared bend down towards her and whisper something to her that made her laugh still more. The music changed and she was swept away in the arms of another partner. Jared stood looking after her, evidently waiting to claim her once more at the first opportunity, Emma thought.

She started to dance with Terry, thinking that they would greet their hostess when this one ended, but it was a dance in which partners interchanged and Emma was soon swept away from Terry. It seemed to go on and on. She felt unable to cope with the light chatter of strange partners in her present mood, and at last she slipped away from the brilliant room and found her way into the quiet garden.

How different it was now from the springtime when she arrived in Africa. She remembered the scent of the orange blossom, the rich romantic fragrance that was all around her when she had realized the fatal joy of Jared's kisses. Now as she walked in the lonely garden of his homestead, with the laughter of the crowd and the music of the dance as distant as a dream that had ended, the bitter smell of autumn filled her with grief and a longing for something that could never be. She did not know how much time passed as she lingered in the darkness. She must go back to Terry, she thought, and she must face the crowd and steel herself to go up to Jared and Yolande and try to be sincere as she wished them happiness. Trying to get up her courage, she went back on the patio. The people who had been sitting here had disappeared inside and she could hear that some kind of speech was being made, for there was laughter and applause. She looked for Terry, but he was on the other side of the room surrounded by some of his men friends. He must have tired of waiting for her, and she could hardly blame him.

'What are you doing here, Emma?'

She swung around and found Jared beside her. For a moment she was breathless with the realization that the man of whom she had been dreaming was actually here by her side.

'Why . . . why aren't you in there?' she asked.

'Why should I be? I've been spending a frustrated evening waiting for you to arrive. When I saw Terry over there with his pals, I finally gave up hope of your coming. I was just going to phone the house when I saw you out here.' His hard expression softened as he looked at her. 'But now you've come, it was worth the waiting. I've never seen you looking so lovely before.'

'But, Jared . . .' Emma could not take in what he was saying, she felt so bewildered, 'shouldn't you be over there with Yolande? They're making speeches.'

'Of course they're making speeches, but they won't miss us, Emma. Now come out into the garden with me and tell me why you arrived so late.'

'I've no intention of coming out with you, Jared. You must be crazy! You should be with Yolande. Even you couldn't take another woman into the garden when your engagement is about to be announced.'

He put his arm around her and against her will she found herself walking with him to the edge of the patio and then down the moss-covered steps. He did not stop until they were beneath the trees. A burst of cheering from the house was followed by the sound of singing in rather discordant notes.

'You can't stay here with me,' Emma protested, completely panic-stricken by now. 'They're cheering and shouting for you. Please go. You must be there – it's important.'

'I agree with you,' he said. 'It is important when you decide to marry someone. And when that happens, Emma, I assure you I'll be there.'

He took her chin in his hands and began to kiss her softly. She wanted to turn away, but the realization swept over her that this was possibly the last time he would ever kiss her. She clung to him, kissing him back, and when it was over, in the darkness she sensed that he was smiling. But he gave a sigh.

'That's better! That's my lovely Emma. Now I've had enough of this running away. I'm not having any more of it. Admit it, obstinate redheaded woman. Say that you love me.'

'What are you asking, Jared? You couldn't be so cruel. It's Yolande who should be saying she loves you.'

'Forget Yolande, Emma, and tell me the truth. If you deny it, I'll go away tomorrow and you need never see me again.'

'You wouldn't do that!' she pleaded.

'Indeed I would. I'll catch a plane to South America

tomorrow if you won't do as I say.'

Emma felt as if she had been asked to jump off a precipice.

'You're a terrible tyrant,' she said. 'You always have been. I don't know how I tolerate you.'

'Say it, Emma, say it,' Jared insisted.

There was something in his voice that she had never heard before, and all at once she knew.

'Very well, then,' she sighed. 'You're the most hateful man that I've ever known, Jared, and I love you more than I can say.'

He swept her into his arms, his head came down to her and he was laughing with joy.

'And I love you, my dearest, sweetest Emma, red-headed temperament and all.' He lifted his head again. 'By the way, before I start kissing you and can't stop, Yolande is marrying one of her Australians and Craig is delighted. They're going back very soon and we can take over the farm again.'

'But I thought . . .'

'You must have been leading the life of a hermit in the last few months. Didn't you know about Yolande? If not, you're about the only person in the district who didn't.'

'I thought you loved her,' she insisted.

'Oh, Emma, how could you think that, when all the time you've been driving me wild with love for you? To-night I made up my mind that I could stand it no longer, that I must forget my age, forget your denials. You must say you'll marry me, my loved one, the sooner the better. If not I feel I shall seize you up in my arms and carry you away.'

'I think there are easier ways of marrying,' said Emma.

Quite a long while afterwards, she said thoughtfully, 'Rosie will be pleased.'

'So you're going to marry me to please Rosie,' Jared grinned. 'Now there's a fine thing!'

'To please Rosie, to please you, to please all the world,' said Emma. 'But most of all to please myself.'

They were married by special licence in the small grey stone church that had been built by early settlers a hundred and fifty years before. The deeply recessed windows were filled with tawny chrysanthemums and bright cotoneaster berries, but they were not as bright as the bride's hair, even under the creamy lace veil that she had found carefully packed away in an old tin trunk brought by some long-ago ancestor. Her dress too was of Edwardian style and lace frilled the sleeves and neck.

They travelled to a holiday house belonging to a sugar farmer friend of Jared's on the Zululand coast. It overlooked a vast stretch of golden coastline and here they spent the first weeks of their marriage, alone and very much in love. Here it was still like summer and sometimes they would drive to small restaurants at seaside resorts and dine on strange delicious seafoods, grilled langoustines or crayfish fresh from the sea. But often they preferred to make a fire on the beach, and Jared would grill their meat to perfection while Emma would occupy herself making a salad and filling pale green avocado pear flesh with delicious prawns.

After one such evening, they had made love and slept and awakened again to the sound of the murmuring sea below their window, the rustle of palm fronds and the small tree frogs shouting for rain.

'Are you awake, my loved one?' asked Jared softly. His arm was around her, her head on his bare shoulder. 'Happy?' he asked her.

'So very happy,' she said. 'I never knew until now that life could be so beautiful.'

'I too,' he said.

They were quiet for a while, utterly at peace, the sound of the waves lulling them back into a rapturous dream.

'When did you first realize that you loved me?' asked Emma, as hundreds of lovers have asked before her.

'I think I knew almost at once that first time we met, but I was slow to recognize it. You said I wasn't afraid of anything, but, Emma my darling, I was afraid of you,' he confessed.

She moved and scanned his face, that now was so infinitely dear to her.

'How could you be afraid of me?' she asked.

'You were so young, so innocent. I was afraid that if I took the love you offered you would be quickly disillusioned. So I shrugged off my own feelings as if they were of no account. I was a fool too. At that time I valued my freedom. I was scared of the deeper emotions you aroused in me. But after you'd gone . . . when I came back and realized that you'd vanished from my life, I felt as if I'd thrown away something infinitely precious. I never really got over it.'

'You have it back again now,' said Emma. 'You have all my love for ever.'

'My sweet beloved,' his low voice was adoring her, 'I was overjoyed when it seemed I'd been given a second chance and your uncle asked me to help you run the farm. But you were so lovely and I thought I was too old for you. You kept declaring you disliked me, then Terry came along and I thought you were interested in him because he was nearer your own age. That's why I seized the excuse to leave you. I couldn't stand it any more.'

'No man has ever made me feel as you do, my own darling,' she said softly. 'I was afraid too, afraid of my own desires, but now you've taught me this, to be proud of love, to feel gloriously, rapturously fulfilled.'

They whispered together, recalling as lovers do the way they had found each other, and then, with the sea sounding in the gentle rhythm of an incoming tide, held in each other's arms, they slept once more.

romance is beautiful!

and Harlequin Reader Service is your passport to the Heart of Harlequin

Harlequin is the world's leading publisher of romantic fiction novels. If you enjoy the mystery and adventure of romance, then you will want to keep up to date on all of our new monthly releases—eight brand new Romances and four Harlequin Presents.

If you are interested in catching up on exciting and valuable back issues, Harlequin Reader Service offers a wide choice of best-selling novels reissued for your reading enjoyment.

If you want a truly jumbo read and a money-saving value, the Harlequin Omnibus offers three intriguing novels under one cover by one of your favorite authors.

To find out more about Harlequin, the following information will be your passport to the Heart of Harlequin.

the omnibus

A Great Idea! Three great romances by the same author, in one deluxe paperback volume.

A Great Value! Almost 600 pages of pure entertainment for only $1.95 per volume.

Essie Summers

Bride in Flight (#933)
...begins on the eve of Kirsty's wedding with the strange phone call that changed her life. Blindly, instinctively Kirsty ran.— but even New Zealand wasn't far enough to avoid the complications that followed!

Postscript to Yesterday (#1119)
...Nicola was dirty, exasperated and a little bit frightened. She was in no shape after her amateur mechanics on the car to meet any man, let alone Forbes Westerfield. He was the man who had told her not to come.

Meet on My Ground (#1326)
...is the story of two people in love, separated by pride. Alastair Campbell had money and position — Sarah Macdonald was a girl with pride. But pride was no comfort to her at all after she'd let Alastair go!

Jean S. MacLeod

The Wolf of Heimra (#990)
...Fenella knew that in spite of her love for the island, she had no claim on Heimra yet — until an heir was born. These MacKails were so sure of themselves; they expected everything to come their way.

Summer Island (#1314)
...Cathie's return to Loch Arden was traumatic. She knew she was clinging to the past, refusing to let it go. But change was something you thought of happening in other places — never in your own beloved glen.

Slave of the Wind (#1339)
...Lesley's pleasure on homecoming and meeting the handsome stranger quickly changed to dismay when she discovered that he was Maxwell Croy — the man whose family once owned her home. And Maxwell was determined to get it back again.

Susan Barrie

Marry a Stranger (#1034)
... if she lived to be a hundred, Stacey knew she'd never be more violently in love than she was at this moment. But Edouard had told her bluntly that he would never fall in love with her!

Rose In the Bud (#1168)
... One thing Cathleen learned in Venice: it was highly important to be cautious when a man was a stranger and inhabited a world unfamiliar to her. The more charm he possessed, the more wary she should be!

The Marriage Wheel (#1311)
... Admittedly the job was unusual — lady chauffeur to Humphrey Lestrode; and admittedly Humphrey was high-handed and arrogant. Nevertheless Frederica was enjoying her work at Farthing Hall. Then along came her mother and beautiful sister, Rosaleen, to upset everything.

Violet Winspear

Beloved Tyrant (#1032)
... Monterey was a beautiful place to recuperate. Lyn's job was interesting. Everything, in fact, would have been perfect, Lyn Gilmore thought, if it hadn't been for the hateful Rick Corderas. He made her feel alive again!

Court of the Veils (#1267)
... In the lush plantation on the edge of the Sahara, Roslyn Brant tried very hard to remember her fiancé and her past. But the bitter, disillusioned Duane Hunter refused to believe that she ever was engaged to his cousin, Armand.

Palace of the Peacocks (#1318)
... Suddenly the island, this exotic place that so recently had given her sanctuary, seemed an unlucky place rather than a magical one. She must get away from the cold palace and its ghost — and especially from Ryk van Helden.

Isobel Chace

The Saffron Sky (#1250)
... set in a tiny village skirting the exotic Bangkok, Siam, the small, nervous Myfanwy Jones realizes her most cherished dream, adventure and romance in a far-off land. Two handsome men determine to marry her, but both have the same mysterious reason. ...

A Handful of Silver (#1306)
... in exciting Rio de Janeiro, city of endless beaches and skyscraper hotels, a battle of wits is waged between Madelaine Delahaye, Pilar Fernandez, the jealous fiancée of her childhood friend, and her handsome, treacherous cousin — Luis da Maestro. ...

The Damask Rose (#1334)
... Vicki Tremaine flies to the heady atmosphere of Damascus to meet Adam Templeton, fiancé of the rebellious Miriam. But alas, as time passes, Vicki only becomes more attracted to this young Englishman with the steel-like personality. ...

information please

**All the Exciting News from
Under the Harlequin Sun**

It costs you nothing to receive our news bulletins and intriguing brochures. From our brand new releases to our money-saving 3-in-1 omnibus and valuable best-selling back titles, our information package is sure to be a hit. Don't miss out on any of the exciting details. Send for your Harlequin INFORMATION PLEASE package today.